The Sheriff

Charles C. Fletcher

2010
Parkway Publishers, Inc.
Boone, North Carolina

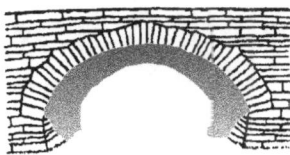

Published by
Parkway Publishers, Inc.
PO Box 3678
Boone, North Carolina 28607
Ph. & Fax: (828) 265-3993

www.parkwaypublishers.com

ACKNOWLEDGMENTS

The author wishes to thank his son Gary Fletcher for editing the typescript of *The Sheriff*. The Reverend Bruce Cayton provided the photograph for the book cover.

FOREWORD

During the early twentieth century, the Sheriff was the most important elected county official in the rural South. This was true in the 1920s and 1930s in Haywood County, North Carolina. Even today, the person who holds the office of the Sheriff wields lot of power in the county where he serves.

This story, *The Sheriff*, is about such a person in the small County of Haywood, nestled in the mountains of Western North Carolina. His life was not an easy one by any means, but he was a first-class citizen, and all who lived in Haywood County and the surrounding counties respected and admired him for upholding the law and keeping the county a safe place to live and raise their families in.

It was the custom of the mountain people to replace the retiring Sheriff with one of his sons. This never was a problem unless the Sheriff who was retiring didn't have a son. In this story, all the Sheriff's children were girls. To carry on the tradition, he had to find himself a son. The Sheriff decided that a son-in-law was close enough, so he began looking for a future husband for one of his girls. This is where our story begins.

Charles Fletcher, Author

July 2010

THE OLD SHERIFF

Paul Harbin was Sheriff of Haywood County, North Carolina, and had been since 1930. He had replaced his father, Buck Harbin, who had been the Sheriff for thirty years, when Buck became old and couldn't get about to carry out the duties of his office. This "keeping it in the family" was a Southern tradition.

Buck Harbin didn't get the Sheriff's job from his father. His father was never the Sheriff of Haywood County. The Sheriff before Buck, Bill Henson, did not have a son. All six of his children were girls. When "Old Bill" was nearing eighty years of age he began looking for someone to take his place.

"I know what I'll do," Old Bill said to himself. "I'll find a good young man and marry off one of my daughters to him. He will then be my son-in-law, and I'll keep the Sheriff's job in the family."

A young fellow by the name of Buck Harbin, Paul

Harbin's future Dad, had been visiting Old Bill quite a bit, not to see Bill but to see his daughters. He was looking over the Henson girls because he was nearing the age for marriage and was looking for a prospect to become his wife. He had never given any thought to the Sheriff's job. All that interested him was one of the Henson girls. He had no idea what Old Bill was planning for his future.

Buck had two choices among the Henson girls. These were the two youngest ones who were unmarried. He picked out the one named Helen. She was the youngest of the Henson girls. She was nearly seventeen years old, and she didn't want to take any chance of being an "old maid," so when Buck asked her to marry him, she said yes, and they set a date for their wedding.

Everything was going as Old Bill had planned. He was getting rid of another daughter; he was getting the son that he had always wanted, and he had found someone to take his place as Sheriff of Haywood County. He only had one more thing to do. That was to get the voters to elect his new son-in-law their Sheriff in the next county election.

"This may take some doing," he thought. "Everyone knows that I am planning on retiring, and there are at least four men who will be running for Sheriff. I've got to get busy. Buck is going to need all the help he can get to win this Sheriff's race. Neither he nor his family had ever been involved in politics, and he is not as well-known as the three other candidates. But I've got a few cards up my sleeve that I can use."

After the wedding was over, all the neighbors pitched in and helped with building a log house for the newlyweds. Old Bill had a few of the prisoners from the County Workhouse help with the building.

The house was soon finished. Buck and Helen bought a few pieces of furniture and moved into their own house. They were their own boss. No one was going to tell Buck how to run his home.

Buck and Helen had been alone only one week when Old Bill, Helen's Dad, who was the High Sheriff of the county, paid them a visit. This was the first step in Bill's plan to have his new son-in-law be the next Sheriff of Haywood County.

After a hug for his daughter and a hand-shake for Buck, Bill invited his son-in-law to go sit in the shade under the big maple tree near the spring. Bill cut himself a big chew of "Apple Tobacco," and offered Buck a chew.

"Better not," Buck said. "I made Helen a promise not to ever take up the habit of tobacco. She said that it was nasty. By now she should have been used to it seeing you chewing and smoking your pipe for all these years. If I don't start chewing, I won't have to quit."

Bill said, "You're going to need a steady job now that you have your own home, and it shouldn't be long before you start having some children to feed." "Yes sir," he said, "You need a regular job." Bill continued, "I guess you have heard that I am retiring from the Sheriff's job after this term. Why don't you run for the job? I think you would be a good replacement. I've been the Sheriff for over forty years, but old age has caught up with me, and I can't get around like I used to."

"I've never given any thought to being a Sheriff and, besides, most people in Haywood County have never heard of me. There are already three men signed up for the election, and they're already putting up their pictures all over the county. It would be a good job, but I would be wasting my time to run."

"You go down to the Courthouse the first thing tomorrow and get your name in the pot for this Sheriff's job. I have a few friends in high places who will help me get the votes that you will need. You just start going around all over the county telling everybody who you are and that you want them to vote for you. You can leave the rest to me. I'll get this job for you."

Buck went to the Courthouse and signed the papers that would make him an official candidate for Sheriff. He started his campaigning as soon as the papers were checked and he was told that he was officially on the ballot. He went into every office in the Courthouse and told them who he was: Buck Harbin, the son-in-law of Bill Henson, the High Sheriff of the county. He also informed them that he was running for the Office of Sheriff and that he was counting on them for their votes.

While young Buck Harbin was paying every family in Haywood County a visit asking for their votes on Election Day, Old Bill was making sure his new son-in-law got the Sheriff's job. In the many years that he had been Sheriff, he had met almost everyone in the county. He had called on them when they broke the law. Some were involved in larger crimes such as fighting, drunkenness from drinking too much moonshine, running a still making moonshine, stealing, and other violations of law.

Bill was often called on to speak to the PTA, the local garden club, and other civic organizations. This was where he would use his influence to get votes for Buck. He wasn't bashful about telling them all the favors he had done for them and how it was their bounden duty to repay him by voting for his son-in-law.

"You elect Buck as your Sheriff, and I can guarantee you that he will carry on as Sheriff the same way I have for all these years past. I'll promise you that he will be a good and fair Sheriff."

Old Bill knew how to get the votes. He had used these same methods when he was up for re-election.

The big day was to be the first Tuesday in May. That was one week away, and Buck was getting a little nervous. He was looking forward to being elected. Not only would this give him a steady, paying job, but he would have the respect of everyone in the county.

"The other ones who are running have posters with their pictures and promises on them hung on trees and buildings all over the county," he said to Bill. "We never put up the first sign."

"We talked to people, and they are the ones who do the voting, not all them fancy signs. Don't you worry," Old Bill assured Buck. "The votes you need will be there when all the votes are counted. Nothing beats a good face-to-face talk with the voters. If they promise you their vote, you will get that vote. The people of Haywood County never go back on their promises. Go home and get some rest. I'll bet that Helen is kind of getting lonesome up there on that mountain with you being gone all day. Go on home. I'll take care of everything from now until Election Day."

Buck did as his father-in-law said. He would stay at home until the day of the election.

When it was the day of the election, Buck went to the Courthouse to meet Bill. They were going to visit all the polling places. Buck would shake some hands, but he would let Old Bill do all the talking.

Bill made it a point to introduce Buck to everyone and brag about what a fine son-in-law he had. This made Buck a little nervous, but he always managed to smile.

After a long twelve-hour day, the polling places closed, and all the ballots were taken to the Courthouse to be counted. The counting was done by hand, and the tally would take several hours to finish. Buck was tired and wanted to go home, but Bill made him stay until the votes were counted and the winner was announced.

It was twelve midnight when the winner was announced. For Bill it was no surprise. His new son-in-law won by a very large margin.

"You can go home now," Bill said to Buck. "The swearing-in will be at the next County Commissioners' meeting. I'll let you know when they will be meeting.

THE NEW SHERIFF

Now that Paul Harbin's dad, Buck Harbin, was retired after many years as the Sheriff of Haywood County, the job was passed on to him as was the custom. He had to prove to the people that he would carry out the duties of the Sheriff's Office the same way his dad did and the others who were Sheriff before his dad.

His first duty was to visit the hardware store, the Café, and the other business places in town. Next were all the meetings that the women had and the clubs that the men belonged to. This was to let them know that he was there to help them when they needed any legal or social advice. Also, this would make his job as Sheriff a lot easier for him if everyone was his friend and they were there to help him when he needed them.

The second thing his dad told him to do was to visit all the families who lived in the hollers and on the ridges of the mountains that surrounded the county seat of

Haywood County.

To be a good Sheriff he had to let everyone know that they could trust him and depend on whatever he told them. He had to become a part of their family.

Once he had all the ground work finished that a good Sheriff needed to make his job easy, he went to his office in the Courthouse, sat in his soft swivel chair, and put his feet on the desk.

"Best job in the county", he said to himself.

But the new Sheriff didn't get to enjoy the peace and quiet that he had hoped for. The door opened and one of the boys who spent most of his time hanging around town hollered out, "Better get over to the blacksmith shop. There is a big fight between one of the Ledbetter boys and Andy Henson. Andy is lots bigger than that puny little Ledbetter boy, and he may kill him if you don't stop their fighting. Don't know what started it, but the both are shore mad. I would guess it's over that Smith girl. Both of them have been courting her. Don't see why they would fight over her. She is the ugliest one of the Smith girls. My eye would be on the middle one. She is nearly sixteen and as pretty as a pup."

The Sheriff took his feet off the desk, stood up, fastened on his gun belt, and left the office. When he arrived at the blacksmith shop everything was quiet. Everyone was standing around as if nothing had happened. The Ledbetter boy and Andy Henson were brushing the dirt off their clothes and rubbing their bruises.

"I guess you won the right to be Ann's boyfriend," the Ledbetter boy said. "I'll not see her any more. Probably pick out one of the other girls."

The two boys then shook hands and left the lot.

"Nothing to this Sheriff's job," Paul said. "It's lots better than chopping wood and plowing." He cocked his hat to one side, smiled, and headed back to his office.

Everything was quiet around the Sheriff's Office, and Paul Harbin was enjoying the many free meals that the local women's clubs were feeding him when he attended their meetings as their guest speaker. He usually used the same speech every time at all the meetings: what a fine group they were; what a great job they were doing; the people couldn't get along without them. He would also make sure to complement the chair-person on her leadership.

The speeches he gave had to be a bit different when he spoke to the men at the Lodge and at other men's gatherings he was invited to as a guest. At these places he didn't get all the good eats that the women's organizations fed him. He was usually served cold-cut sandwiches and soft drinks. Of course, there would be some good moonshine before the meetings for those who needed something to help them relax from their hard day's work. The moonshine also made the cold-cuts taste better. Paul usually passed up the liquor at these gatherings, although he did have a few drinks sometimes when he was at home.

After one of the Lodge meetings, Bill Henson, one of the members, was waiting outside the Lodge. When Paul came out Bill put his hand on the Sheriff's shoulder and said. "Sheriff, I need to have a talk with you".

"Fine," the Sheriff said. "What's on your mind?"

"The last time you visited me you were admiring my flock of chickens. You know that I depend on them for a little extra money. I usually take about ten dozen eggs to the stores in town every Saturday. Well, lately I've not been getting as many eggs as I did, so I figured that something was wrong. Monday evening after the chickens went to roost, I counted the hens. There were ten fewer hens than I had a month ago. It's easy to see why I was short on eggs. Ten hens laying one egg a day times seven days — that's over five dozen eggs a week I'm losing. I believe that someone is stealing my chickens," Bill said.

Paul said, "I'll check around and let you know if I find out anything in a few days. Better put a lock on the chicken house. If someone is getting your hens, it would be at night. Don't think they could catch them in the day time."

Bill left the office, and Paul put his feet back up on his desk, leaned back in his chair, and took a nap.

A few days later, Bill Henson stopped by the Sheriff's Office.

"Sheriff," Bill said. "You can stop looking for the chicken thief. Last night the chickens woke me up about ten o'clock. They were squawking to the top of their lungs. I got a flashlight and my shotgun and went out to see what had them so upset. When I opened the chicken house door, out came the biggest red fox I have ever seen. I let him have both barrels of that 12 gauge gun: blew half of his head off. He must have been eating my hens. Thanks for looking into it anyway."

A MURDER

Sheriff Paul Harbin was getting his daily nap in his easy chair behind his desk when Bob Boyd came rushing in shouting.

"Sheriff, you got to help me! I can't put up with that woman much longer."

"Hold it! Hold it!" Paul said. "Calm down and tell me what your problem is. Can't make heads or tails of what you are talking about the way you are carrying on."

Bob sat down in the chair in front of the Sheriff's desk and began. "Well, Sheriff," he began. "I guess you heard that I got married about six months ago. I couldn't find me a woman around here, so I went over the mountain to Haysville. One of my buddies was telling me about a family over there that had five girls and none of them married. They go by the name of 'Ensley'.

"Sure enough, there they were: five real pretty girls, all smiling and giggling. I spent the whole day talking to them before I picked out the one I thought would make me a good wife. Then I asked Mr. Ensley, the girl's dad, if I could marry one of his girls.

11

"'Which one do you want?' he asked me.

"'I think I would like the one with the red hair if she will have me,' I told him.

"'You mean Sally,' he said. 'She would be tickled to be married to you. Go ahead and ask her,' he said.

"Well, Sheriff, that's how I got my wife. I haven't had a minute's peace since the Justice of the Peace married us. I wish I had never got married. I haven't slept in my bed since the day we were married. That woman is as mean as the devil to me if I get anywhere near her. She makes me sleep in the barn. I'm telling you, Sheriff, you got to go talk with her. Tell her it's against the law to treat me like this. If she don't change, I may go way off somewhere so she can't find me -- may even go to somewhere near the ocean."

"You go back home, and I'll drop by in a few days and have a talk with her," the Sheriff said.

"Don't wait too long," Bob said. I don't know how much more I can take. I'd shore appreciate anything you can do. That woman is shore a mean one. It must be that red hair."

A few days later Paul decided to visit Bob Boyd and see how things were going with him and his wife Sally. When he arrived, he knocked on the front door. After several knocks without an answer, he decided that no one was at home. He turned to leave, and, as he turned around, he saw Bob out by the barn. He had a shovel in his hands and seemed to be digging or something. Paul walked to where Bob was working.

"What are you doing?" Paul asked him.

"I'm burying Sally," he said.

"You are doing what?" Paul said.

"Burying my wife," Bob said.

"Tell me what's going on here, Bob," Paul asked.

"Well… You know the other day when I was at your office and asked you to see if you would talk to Sally about the way she was treating me? Things got worse since then. This morning she hit me with an iron skillet. See this big bump on the side of my head? I had to protect myself, so I grabbed my shotgun and shot her square in the face. She didn't holler or nothing. She just fell over in the floor. After thinking for a few minutes I decided that I'd better bury her. That's what I'm doing, Sheriff: Giving her a decent burial. I may find some flowers for her grave when I get her covered up."

"I guess you know that I'll have to arrest you for murder," Paul said.

"It wasn't murder, Sheriff. It was self defense," Bob said.

"When you finish burying her, you come on in to my office. I've got to lock you up."

"I'll be there," Bob said.

The Sheriff left Bob and headed back to town. He knew that Bob would keep his word and turn himself in as soon as he finished filling the grave and putting up some kind of a tombstone or marker.

THE TRIAL

Bob had been in jail for two weeks when a date was set for his trial. The Prosecutor hadn't bothered to prepare a strong case against Bob because it was a clear case of murder. He wouldn't have any trouble proving that Bob committed murder when he addressed the jurors.

Bob had requested that the Sheriff be a witness for his defense. The court appointed a lawyer to represent Bob, and the twelve jurors were picked. The trial would begin as soon as the Judge arrived.

This was the biggest thing that had happened in Haywood County since the government was getting all the Cherokee Indians together to send them out west. The local schools were closed for the trial, and some of the stores were closed for the day. Almost everyone wanted to be in the courtroom when the trial was in session.

Everyone was enjoying the event except poor old Bob. He was as nervous as he had been on his wedding day. Bob and the Sheriff were sitting on a bench directly in front of where the Judge would be seated.

"Don't worry," the Sheriff said to Bob. "You will get

to speak your piece before the jurors and the Judge. Everything will be OK."

The Judge came into the courtroom, and everyone stood until he sat down. The Court Deputy called the court to order and announced that it was in session. Bob was asked to stand before the Judge.

The Court Clerk read the charges against Bob. "Bob Boyd, you are charged with first degree murder. What is your plea?"

"Not guilty, Your Judgeship," Bob said. "I wouldn't have shot her if she hadn't hit me with that iron skillet."

"Take your seat, Mr. Boyd," the Judge said. "Your turn will come, and then you can tell the court what happened."

"The Prosecution will present their case," the Judge said.

"Your Honor, I'll introduce myself to the jurors. My name is Will Williams from the law office of Williams, Williams, and Williams. I'm going to prove that this man, Bob Boyd, killed his poor wife without any justified reason. He is a cold-blooded murderer."

"I am not," Bob said. "If I hadn't shot her, she would have killed me with that frying pan. Don't call me a murderer."

"Mr. Boyd, sit down, and do not interrupt this trial again," said the Judge.

"I would like to have the defendant to take the witness stand, Your Honor."

"Mr. Boyd, please be sworn in and take the witness stand," said the Judge.

"Raise your right hand," said the Court Deputy.

"I, Bob Boyd, do swear to tell the whole truth, so help

me God," Bob said.

"Sit down," the Deputy said.

Lawyer Williams had his hand on his chin and was pacing back and forth in front of Bob. He would look at him every time he got in front of him, but he never said anything.

"Judge, make him quit walking back and forth in front of me. He's making me nervous," Bob said.

"Mr. Boyd, don't speak until you are asked to," the Judge said.

"Well, make him start asking," .Bob said. "He's stalking me like I was a bear or some other animal."

"Do you have any questions you would like to ask the defendant?" the Judge asked Lawyer Williams.

"Did you kill your wife"?

"I shot her after she hit me with that frying pan. I guess that's what killed her."

"And were you in the process of burying her when the Sheriff came to your house?"

"If you shot your wife, would you let her lie around the house until she began to stink?"

"Just answer with a 'yes' or 'no', Mr. Boyd," the Judge said.

"And you admit that you killed her?"

"Yes."

"I have no more questions, Your Honor."

"You can step down, Mr. Boyd."

Sheriff Harbin got up from his seat and approached the Judge. He whispered something to the Judge and returned to his seat.

"We will take a twenty-minute break," the Judge said, and he hit the top of his desk with a wooden hammer.

The Sheriff followed the Judge into an adjoining room and shut the door. When the twenty minutes were over, the Judge returned and took his seat.

"The Prosecutor will address the jurors now," the Judge said.

Lawyer Williams began walking back and forth in front of the jurors like he did in front of Bob when he was in the witness chair. He didn't say a word; he just stared.

Finally, he said to the jury, "You all have heard what the defendant said. There is no question that Bob Boyd killed his wife and that he is nothing but a cold-blooded murder. You only have one choice when you make your decision: That is, he is guilty of first degree murder."

Lawyer Williams returned to his seat.

Sheriff Harbin got up from his seat and said, "Your Honor, I would like to say something to the jury."

"You may," the Judge said.

The Sheriff approached where the jurors were seated and began speaking. "All of you have known me ever since I was a small boy. You know my family, and you know that I would never tell you anything but the truth. Well, this may sound a little strange, but I feel that I had a little to do with Bob's killing his wife. Not only had I heard about the way she treated him from his neighbors, but Bob had come to my office and asked me to go talk with her. He said that he had slept in the barn ever since they were married. He had to sneak into the house to get something to eat.

"Well, I kept putting off paying them a visit, and when I did go, it was too late. I found Bob burying his wife, Sally. So you see, maybe if I had done my duty and gone sooner this would not have happened.

"I have known the Boyd family all my life, and they are a fine family. None of them has ever been in any kind of trouble. When you make your decision on this case, I ask you to look at all the facts before passing judgment. Put yourself in Bob's shoes and ask yourself what you would have done."

The Sheriff returned to his seat and the jury left the courtroom.

"We'll take a half-hour break," said the Judge.

Bob put his hand on the Sheriff's shoulder and said, "Sheriff, if I had known that I was causing all this much trouble, I would have never killed Sally. I would have left the country. Maybe I'd have gone to China."

"Calm down. Things will work out all right. Let's go get a cup of coffee."

When Bob and the Sheriff returned to the courtroom, it was packed. There was not an empty seat. Bob and the Sheriff returned to the seats that they sat in during the trial.

The Judge returned to his seat behind the dais and called the Court Deputy to come forward. "Go to the jury room and ask the Foreman if they have reached a decision," he instructed the Deputy.

When he returned, the jurors were behind him, and they took their seats in the jurors' box.

The Judge asked, "Have the jurors reached a decision?"

The Jury Foreman stood and said, "We have, Your Honor. We find the defendant guilty of second degree murder. We also recommend that the defendant receive a minimum sentence when you make your decision."

Everyone in the court room began to whisper. The

Judge hit the top of his desk with his gavel. "The court will come to order!"

When the noise stopped, the Judge began, "This has been the strangest case I have ever heard. I am inclined to agree with the jurors' decision. This was more like self defense than murder. The defendant will approach the bench."

Bob didn't move. The Sheriff nudged him with his elbow and said, "Go on. That's you."

The judge began, "Bob Boyd, I sentence you to six months in prison and a twelve-month suspended sentence after you have served the time in prison. The sentence will be served in the county jail here in Haywood County. A word of advice for you: If you marry again, you had better take a little more time to get acquainted with the woman and look for her bad habits first. This court is adjourned."

Charles C. Fletcher

BAD MOONSHINE

It was quiet around the jail since the "big trial", and the Sheriff was glad to have Bob as a prisoner in his jail. Not only was Bob a good checker player, he also kept the jail and office clean.

The Sheriff's job was back to normal. Only a few family squabbles and a few fights were all he had to attend to over the past two months. With this and a few social meetings with the local clubs, all he was doing other than playing checkers with Bob was catching a few naps every now and then. The Sheriff's job was the best of all the county offices.

This "easy life" was about to end for Paul. He received a call asking him to come to the hospital. The doctor wanted to talk with him.

"It's urgent," the caller said. "Get here as soon as you can."

The Sheriff told Bob to go back to his cell and lock the

door until he returned. Bob put away the checker board, went to his cell, closed the door and went to his bunk.

"Think I'll take a little nap. The Sheriff may not be gone too long, and when he comes back the first thing to do is finish the checker game."

The hospital was about a mile from the Courthouse and jail and too far to walk, so the Sheriff cranked up the Model-A Ford that he used for the official duties of the Sheriff. He was real careful not to take the car anywhere that he thought it may get a scratch or dent. He would always park it at the foot of the mountain when he was looking for moonshine stills or during any other business he had off the main road. As Sheriff, this car was a big benefit for him. He got a lot of attention when he was driving this "black beauty", especially when he would use the "oogah" horn to warn everybody to get out of his way.

When he arrived at the hospital, Doctor Stone, the Doctor who had asked for him, was waiting at the receiving desk in the emergency room.

"Sheriff, old Willie, the town drunk, is in terrible shape. He must have got ahold of some of that Georgia likker. I hear that they make it in their turpentine stills and use old car radiators instead of a worm. Everybody knows that them radiators are mostly lead, and lead is deadly poison. You'd better find out where he got this moonshine before he passes on."

The Doctor led the way to Willie's room and the Sheriff followed close behind him.

"Sheriff, this is Willie. I'll leave and you can talk to him."

The Doctor left the room, and Sheriff Harbin pulled a

chair to the side of the bed and sat down.

"Willie," the Sheriff began. "The Doctor told me that you had a bad case of poisoning. He said that it was from something that you had drunk. It's very important that you tell me what you drank before you came to the hospital. Whatever it was and wherever you got it is very important. You can keep someone else from ending up in the graveyard if you tell me and I can get rid of whatever it is and stop the person who has it from letting others get hold of it."

"Well, Sheriff, you know I like my likker, and I don't work very much, so I have to buy the cheapest likker I can find. What I've been drinking cost me a dollar for a half gallon. I got it from a feller up in the other end of the county."

"Who is this fellow, Willie?" the Sheriff asked.

"Guess you may have heard of him," Willie said. "He goes by the name of 'Hoss'. He probably got the name from being a horse trader." He lives up by the river in Beaverdam section. That's where all the black people live. He's black and sort of a self-appointed leader of the black community. He sells as much likker to white people as he does to the blacks. That's all I know, Sheriff."

"Thanks Willie. I don't know exactly where he lives, but I'll find him before the sun goes down today."

The Sheriff got up and left the room. He drove the Ford back to his office at the courthouse. When he opened the door he looked around for Bob. He didn't see him up front, so he went to the jail section. There he was on one of the bunks in the cell, the door locked, and the keys lying on the little table by the bed.

"Bob!" the Sheriff hollered. "Wake up!"

Bob jumped to his feet, rubbed his eyes, and looked around to see who was calling him. "Sheriff," he said. "I didn't plan on sleeping all evening. When did you get back?"

Sheriff Harbin returned to his desk and Bob came into the office from the jail cell.

"Bob, I'll probably be gone the rest of the day, so you sit here at my desk and answer the phone. If anyone calls or if anybody comes by, you get their message and write it down. Tell them I had some urgent business to take care of and that I'll take care of whatever they want as soon as I get back."

"Yes sir," Bob said. "I'll be right here when you return. Sheriff, if it's past suppertime before you get back, what will I do for food?"

"You can go to the Café and get something. Have them charge it to me. Don't get anything that costs a lot. I'll see you when I get back tonight."

The Sheriff didn't usually carry his pistol, but he put the "45" under his belt and left. It was only ten miles to the Beaverdam section of Haywood County. He was driving about thirty miles an hour, so he would be there in about fifteen minutes.

"There's no need to hurry. I've got all evening," he said to himself.

As he turned onto the street where all the black people lived, he noticed that there was only one car on the street. He guessed that the house it was parked in front of would be where Hoss lived. He parked his Ford behind the old Chevy touring car and got out. When he drove up he noticed several small children, but they had disappeared. No one was in sight.

The Sheriff went to the front door of the house and knocked. A lady with a bandana tied around her head opened the door.

"I'm looking for a fellow who goes by the name of Hoss. Can you tell me where I can find him?"

"Yes sir," the lady said. "This is where he lives. His real name is John Gibson, but everybody calls him Hoss. He's taking a nap, but I'll go get him. Who are you?" she asked.

"Tell him that it's the Sheriff but not to get excited. I only need some information from him.

"Sho hope he ain't done nothing to get in trouble with the Law. We got six children to take care of, and if something happened to Hoss, I couldn't make out. Laudy me. I hope he ain't in any trouble."

A big black man about six-foot-six came to the door rubbing his eyes. "Howdy Sheriff. I'm Hoss. The old lady said you wanted to talk with me. Want to come in the house?"

"Hoss, I need to ask you some questions, and I think it would be better that we don't talk where your wife and children can hear. Let's go out to the car and talk."

"Yes sir. Be fine with me."

They stood beside the Sheriff's car while the Sheriff began to ask Hoss some questions.

"Hoss, do you know a fellow by the name of Willie?"

"Yes sir, I do. I saw him yesterday. Is anything wrong with him?"

"Yes, he's in the hospital, and they don't know if he will live through the night."

"Lawdy me. What's wrong with him?"

"Poisoning. He drank some bad likker. Said he got it

from you. Know anything about that likker?"

"Yes, I guess you heard that I do sell a little likker all along. I have to keep my children clothed and fed. Can't find any steady work anywhere. I'm sorry about Ol' Willie. Hope he makes it."

"Hoss, where did you get that whiskey?"

"Well, sir, day before yesterday a man from Georgia come by and had a truck full of likker, all in half-gallon jars. Said he had made more than he could sell in Georgia, so he come to North Carolina to get rid of it. Said he would take fifty cents a jar. That's half the price we pay for 'shine made around here, so I got twelve jars. All I could afford. Didn't have but six dollars."

"Do you know how they make whiskey down in Georgia?"

"No, sir."

"They use old car radiators instead of a worm. These radiators are put together with lead, and the lead gets in the whiskey. That's what poisoned Willie. Lead poisoning. Kills a person nearly every time. How much of that whiskey have you sold?"

"Only the jar that I let Willie have for a dollar. I was saving the other eleven till Saturday. I'll get a dollar and a half then."

"Hoss, if you'll pour out that whiskey and promise me that you'll never get any more whiskey from outside places and try to find a job, I won't arrest you for selling whiskey this time. But if Willie dies, I'll have to come get you for murder. Do you understand?"

"Yes, sir. I sho do. I hope Ol' Willie makes it. I don't know what the ol' woman and children would do if I had to go to the chain gang."

"Go get all the moonshine that you have and bring it out here. I want to be sure you are getting rid of that bad moonshine before I leave."

Hoss was gone just a few minutes before he returned with a box with six half-gallon jars in it.

"Have to get the others," he said.

He returned with five more jars and began to pour their contents onto the ground beside the car. Soon the area began to smell like a bar room. It was pretty strong stuff. The grass in the yard began to wilt as soon as the poison whiskey touched it. Soon all eleven jars were empty.

"Got any more in the house?" the Sheriff asked.

"No, sir. That is all I have."

"You'd better keep your promise to me. If I ever hear of you dealing in bad likker again, I'll come get you and you will serve time on the gang. Better pray that Willie makes it."

"Yes, sir."

"The boss at the tannery is a friend of mine. He needs extra help every now and then. I'll speak to him about you tomorrow. You go see him next week. Mention that I sent you. His name is

Sam Taylor. Maybe he will give you some work and you can quit the whiskey business."

The Sheriff then got into his car and headed back to his office. It had been a busy day for Sheriff Harbin.

THE REVENUERS

Sheriff Harbin didn't frown on or try stopping the making of moonshine in Haywood County until the Federal alcohol agents began to put pressure on him. He didn't see any harm in the poor mountain men selling their corn crop in the liquid form to get money for clothing and feeding their family. There was not much of a demand for corn unless it was in a half-gallon fruit jar. And the Sheriff liked a little drink every once in a while to settle his nerves after a hard day's work.

The Federal agents could not catch the seasoned moonshine haulers. They used a lot of tricks and ways to confuse the lawmen who did everything that they were trained to do to catch the "runners" and send them to prison. When they did trap a car that was supposed to have a load of whiskey, it was always empty. It was a practice for the haulers to use two or more cars all looking exactly alike. When the chase began, the cars would split up and go in different directions. The lawmen always caught up with the one that didn't have any moonshine. The car that had the whiskey was safely on its way to some bootlegger in one of the nearby towns. They also would have a car that was a different model and style hide on a side road, and they would transfer their load and then let the Feds catch them.

The runners also had other tricks that they used. They would equip their cars with tack-nail droppers that they used to cause their followers to have flat tires. They would also have smoke screens to blind their followers. This was done by having a container of old motor oil in the trunk or rumble seat of their car.

To fog up the road with smoke they opened a valve that let the oil flow into the hot part of the car engine. When it burned, it made a black smoke behind the car. They would use children or women as decoys. The cars were equipped with metal shields that were lowered to protect the back tires from shooting to cause the tires to go flat. They were not engineers, and some could only read a little and sign their name, but they did know how to equip their cars.

Sheriff Harbin knew these people and how they earned money in order to feed their families. This was why the Government men asked for his help. The Sheriff agreed to help catch the moonshine haulers if the Feds would do it his way. All the road races and shooting were out. He didn't want anyone to get hurt. He would catch them with a simple plan: a trap.

He sent word through a local bootlegger that he wanted to talk with Jim Clark. Jim was the leader who all the haulers and bootleggers went to for advice. In a round-about way, all of the whiskey business belonged to Jim.

The next day the Sheriff had a visitor. Jim got the message that Sheriff Harbin wanted to talk with him.

"Morning, Sheriff," Jim said. "Got word you wanted to see me".

"Yes, got to talk with you. You already know all the trouble the Feds are causing your boys. They have asked me to help them. I agreed to help, but I need your help. I am sure you want to get rid of them as much as I do. If you will give me a little help, we can send them home and everything will get back to normal around here."

"What you got planned, Sheriff? I'll help all I can. If we don't get this stopped soon, someone is going to get killed racing on these narrow dirt roads at 50 and 60 miles an hour with the Law behind them shooting at their tires. Sure got to get this stopped."

The Sheriff called Bob, the trustee and only prisoner he had in jail. "Bob," the Sheriff said. "Jim and I have some business to talk about. I'll call the County Clerk and tell them you are coming to their office. You stay there until I call you."

As soon as Bob left the room the Sheriff asked Jim to move his chair closer so they wouldn't have to talk loud.

"What we talk about is between you and me. No one is ever to know about this meeting," said the Sheriff.

"What you got in mind?" Jim asked.

"Well, the way I see it these lawmen from Washington are not going to leave here until they catch someone with a load of moonshine. Now if we can find one of the boys who is willing to spend a year in the Federal pen and he will let them catch him, this would solve the problem for everyone. They would move on to another county once they could send in their report that they caught a likker runner and sent him to prison. To find that person is your job. My job will be to give the Feds a plan for catching him."

"Don't right off know which of the boys would do this. I'll have to get them all together and talk it over with them. I'll get back with you before the end of the week."

Jim rose from his chair and left the Sheriff's Office without saying anything else.

Monday morning when the Sheriff arrived at his office, Jim was waiting for him.

"Hello, Jim. Been here long?"

"Since about 7:30. You sleep late on Mondays?" Jim asked the Sheriff.

"No. Never come to work until eight unless it's an emergency."

"Got some good news," Jim said. "One of the Pressley boys volunteered to let the Revenuers catch him. He is only eighteen, the oldest of the three boys in the Pressley family. His name is Ben Junior. The other two are called Paul and Sam. All the other whiskey runners agreed to pitch in and pay him while he is in prison. They want the Feds to get out of Haywood County so everything will get back to normal."

"Where does he want them to catch him?"

"Do you know where the Brown Cove Road goes up to the gap of the mountain? He said that would be a good place because the road is narrow and they wouldn't have any trouble blocking it. It'll make them look good, too, seeing as how he wouldn't be able to get away like he had the other times they tried to catch him."

"When does he want this to take place?"

"Tomorrow, Tuesday, right after dinner. About 1:30."

"OK. I'll set everything up with the lawmen. Have to be careful how we handle this. If our plans are discovered, you and I both will go to prison instead of the Pressley boy."

The Sheriff knew that Jim would never tell about his meeting with him. These mountain people were honorable, and if they told you anything, it would always be so. The meeting was over. Neither man spoke. They shook hands, and Jim left the office.

When the Sheriff was sure that Jim was out of town, he put his hat on and headed to what the Washington lawmen called, the 'command post'. They had rented a couple of rooms above the hardware and feed store. The furnishings were a couple of desks and about a half dozen straight-back chairs. Maps of Haywood County were on all four walls with different color thumbtacks stuck on every mountain and road in the entire county.

Bud climbed the long stairs up to the second floor where the command post was. He knocked on the door and a voice said, "Who's there?"

"Paul Harbin, the Sheriff of this county."

"Come on in. The door is unlocked."

He opened the door and saw the man who all the other lawmen called the 'Captain' sitting behind one of the desks.

"What can I do for you?" the Captain asked.

"You want to catch one of the haulers?" the Sheriff said.

"Sure do. Been trying for over a month and haven't

come close. Them boys are pretty sharp not to have any formal education. What do you have on your mind?" he asked.

"Well," the Sheriff said. "I had a drunk in jail yesterday, and he was pretty free with what he knew about the whiskey haulers. He was mad at one of them for charging him what he thought was too much. Said he wished he would get caught.

"I questioned him about this man. He told me he knew the road that he used to keep from getting caught. If you are interested, I'll help you with a plan to ketch him."

The Captain's eyes opened wide as a coon's eyes. He was all excited. He got up from his desk, pulled one of the chairs up close, and asked Paul to have a seat.

"This hauler is one of the Pressley boys. He's just past eighteen years old. He started driving and hauling moonshine when he was about sixteen. He brags a lot about being too smart for you people to catch him. I found out that he always takes the Brown Gap Road. It's just a narrow wagon road, and you people never figured out that it could be used by a car."

"Did you find out when his next run will be?" the Captain asked.

"Yes. Tomorrow between 11:30 and 1:00. I have a plan if you want to hear it."

"Sure do."

"Well, get one of your cars stationed at the gap of the mountain about 11:00 tomorrow. Have your men block the road so nothing can get by. I'll ride in your car with you. We will park beside the Baptist Church on the road leading to the wagon road. When we see the Pressley boy, pass we'll give him time to go get his load, and then we will make sure he can't come out our way."

"Sounds like you have it all worked out." The Captain was all smiles.

"I'll be here at your office around 10:45 tomorrow. No one is to know of our plan except you and me. If the Pressley boy found out, he would postpone the haul."

The next day Sheriff Harbin arrived at the Revenuers' command post at about 10:05, ready to help catch the Pressley boy.

"Better get going," the Captain said to the Sheriff. "Don't want him to get away this time. I've been out-smarted too many times already."

Sheriff Harbin and the Captain got into an unmarked car and went on their way. Two of the other agents were already at the place where they would block the road. The Sheriff and the Captain would park by the Baptist church.

Their wait was not long. At 12:00 an A-model coup came by headed up Brown Cove Road. The Pressley boy saw the car beside the church, but he didn't let on that he knew that it was there and that it would follow him.

Five minutes after the Ford passed, the Sheriff and the Federal Agent started up Brown Cove Road follow-ing behind the Pressley boy. Suddenly they were behind the Ford. It was stopped in the road, and the other two agents were standing in front of it with their guns point-ed toward it.

When the Sheriff and Captain got out, the Pressley boy saw the Sheriff and spoke to him. "Sheriff Harbin, what are you doing here? I never expected you to do a thing like this to me. You know that me and all of my kin voted for you. Why are you helping these people?"

He had his lines well rehearsed. He never wanted the federal agents to suspect that this was all planned.

The agents soon had handcuffs on the Pressley boy, and they led him to their car.

"I'll drive his car back to the Courthouse," said Sheriff Harbin.

He never spoke to the prisoner. He did look his way and thought he saw a smile from him. The plan had worked perfectly. The Federal agents never knew that it was planned.

The prisoner was immediately transferred to the state capital jail where he was given a quick trial and sentenced to the federal prison for a period of one year with one year's probation when he was released.

The Revenuers' office was closed; they had packed all of their maps and other belongings, and were on their way to another county that had a lot of "moonshining activity". Haywood County was now back to normal. Everyone was happy again, including Sheriff Harbin.

THE DEPUTY SHERIFF

Everything was going along pretty smoothly in Haywood County, but the Sheriff seemed to be working harder. There was an increase in family squabbles, chicken stealing, and other disputes that he had to look into and get settled.

"I need someone to help me," he said to himself. He began to make plans. "I'll get me a Deputy," he said to himself.

Bob Boyd was still hanging around the jail although he had finished his jail term for killing his wife. He kept the jail clean, answered the telephone when the Sheriff was gone, and did anything that the Sheriff wanted him to do. He didn't receive any pay, but the Sheriff bought his meals at the local Café and let him sleep in one of the cells at the jail.

Bob and the Sheriff were playing a game of checkers. Between moves the Sheriff asked Bob, "How would you like a full-time job in the Sheriff's Office?"

"What do you mean?" Bob asked

"Well, I need someone to help me run this office. I'm sure that you have noticed that I never have any time to relax like I used to have. I haven't played a game of checkers for over two months now. Been behind in my work ever since them government men were here. Sure glad they are gone."

"You still haven't told me what you have in mind," Bob said.

"I'm going to ask the County Commissioners for money to pay a full-time Deputy to help me keep law and order in Haywood County. They have a meeting planned for next Monday. I'll stop by today and get my name on the list for business at the next meeting. How much pay do you think you would need to work full-time?" the Sheriff asked.

"You can decide what I would be worth. I've never had much money, so I don't think it would take a lot for me to get by. When I worked for someone in the past, they paid me a dollar a day if I worked ten hours."

The Deputy's job was not mentioned again, and the Sheriff was away from the jail most of the time. Bob answered the telephone and kept the jail clean when the Sheriff was gone. The only time he was away was when he went to the Café for something to eat. He charged all his meals to the county jail.

When the County Commissioners had their regular meeting on Monday, the Sheriff was sitting on the front bench in the meeting room. He was ready to ask for the money he needed to hire a full-time Deputy to help him keep law and order in Haywood County.

The Sheriff

The meeting was called to order by the Commission Chairman. He asked everyone to rise, face the United States flag, and say the pledge of allegiance.

After everyone was seated, the Chairman said to the Commissioners, "The first order of business will be a request from Sheriff Harbin."

The Sheriff left his seat and went to the front of the meeting room.

"As you all know, Haywood County is growing real fast. At the last census we had over five thousand people in our county. This has increased the work that I have to do to protect the good people of Haywood County to the point that I need someone to help me. I am asking you Commissioners to increase my budget one hundred dollars a month so I can hire a full-time Deputy.

"Is there any discussion?" the Chairman asked.

Commissioner Smith raised his hand.

"Commissioner Smith is recognized."

"Mr. Chairman, I don't think the good Sheriff needs any help, and that to grant him this extra money would be a waste of our tax dollars."

"Mr. Chairman, can I answer Mr. Smith?"

"You can", said the chairman.

"The person who would be sworn in as a Deputy Sheriff would be responsible for keeping the jail clean in addition to his Deputy's duties."

"I don't think we should waste money on keeping the jail so clean. Prisoners don't need to be pampered," Mr. Smith said.

"Mr. Smith," the Sheriff began. "Last week I was riding my horse in the north section of the county. I came to the branch that runs out of Hickory Cove. I stopped to let my horse have a drink of water from branch. He put his mouth in the water, jerked his head up, shook it and snorted. He wouldn't drink that water. Do you know why? Well it's a known fact that a horse or mule won't drink water if it has any alcohol in it. This means one thing: There is a moonshine still somewhere up that branch. And do you know who lives up that cove? I believe that your sister's house, the sister who married the Ledbetter boy, is the only house up there.

"Now, if the Revenue officers who were here a while back were to come and catch your brother-in-law, and he was put in my jail, and your sister came to visit and saw bugs and rats in his cell, and found out that you don't believe in a clean jail, and you were against having someone keep it clean, what would you tell her if she complained?"

"Mr. Chairman, I have changed my mind. I recommend that we increase the Sheriff's budget so he can have a Deputy."

When the Sheriff returned to his office at the jail, Bob was waiting to hear what had happened at the meeting.

"I got the money. I'm going to see the Judge tomorrow to set a date for a swearing-in ceremony. You will be a full-time paid Deputy starting next week. I'm going to pay you a hundred dollars a month."

"That's a lot of money. Never had that much money in my life. Thank you, Sheriff. I'll do my best to earn it."

After Bob had taken the oath of office, he and the Sheriff went back to the jail. "Bob, here is your badge. I don't have a pistol for you, but I will find one soon."

"Don't need a gun. Don't want to shoot anyone".

"You still have to carry one."

The Sheriff continued to tell Bob what all his duties were. One was keeping the jail clean. If there were prisoners, he would have them do the work, but if there were none, he would do the cleaning. Also, he could continue sleeping at the jail. He would now have to pay for his meals himself.

Everything was taken care of. The Sheriff had a full-time Deputy, and Haywood County now had two full-time employees to enforce the laws and protect the people.

A FUNERAL

Three months had passed since Bob was hired as the first Deputy Sheriff of Haywood County. The Sheriff was spending more time at home now. Bob was covering the county to make sure everyone saw him in his new uniform.

It was not really a uniform -- just a pair of black pants and a blue shirt. No one had ever seen Bob with anything on besides a pair of denim overalls. He was proud of his new clothes. The Sheriff had helped him pick them out at the dry goods store.

One day when he and the Sheriff were playing a game of checkers, he broke the silence. "Sheriff, would it be OK if I took off a couple of days?"

"What for?"

"I thought I might go dig up Sally's body and move it to the graveyard at the Baptist Church. My Daddy bought about twenty lots for our family. There is plenty of room for a grave for Sally. I'm kind of sorry I killed her. I wouldn't have if she hadn't hit me with that iron skillet.

"I guess she is still where I buried her at the barn near my house. Not been back to check. Now that I've got money, I was thinking of buying her a coffin. Just a cheap one."

"I guess I could make out," said the Sheriff. Everybody deserves a decent grave. Just let me know what days you want off."

"I've got to find someone who will loan me a horse and sled. I can't take a wagon up that narrow road. And a car would never get up there. There's only ever been one car made it up that mountain. That was the car that belongs to the Ledbetter boy who lives over in Hickory Holler. He drove his T-model Ford up there once. Well, he *backed* it up. He said the forward clutch was wore out. He won a half gallon of moonshine on a bet with some of the boys he runs around with. They bet him he couldn't do it."

"I'll loan you my horse, but I don't have a sled. Shouldn't be hard to borrow one. Most all the farmers have 'em. I never did any farming, so I never bothered to make one."

The Sheriff cleared his throat and said to Bob, "Bob, how are you going to get Sally out of the ground? You buried her all in one piece. It's been a long time, and I guess there is only a pile of bones left by now."

"There may only be bones, but they'll be all together. I wrapped her in the oil cloth that was on the kitchen table. I tied it up real good with some hay binding twine I had at the barn. I'll pick her up real easy and lay her in the coffin that I'm taking on the sled. I got it all figured out.

"The first thing I got to do is dig the grave at the Baptist Church graveyard. There's a lot of digging in fixing a grave. It's got to be four feet wide by eight feet long and six feet deep. I helped dig my daddy's grave. It took us

41

almost all day to dig it."

When the Sheriff came to the office on Monday morning, Bob met him at the door.

"Sheriff, I found a sled. When I went to the funeral home to buy a coffin for Sally, I told them I would pick it up when I found a sled to haul it on. Guess what? They have a sled at the funeral home. Said they had to use it several times when they went onto one of the mountains after someone who had died. They told me I could borrow it. Could I be off tomorrow and Wednesday?

"I'll dig the grave tomorrow and go get Sally on Wednesday. The Baptist Church people have prayer meetings on Wednesdays, and I may get one of them to say a few words over Sally's grave."

"Things are kind of quiet around here, and I don't have anything planned for the next few days. Take off those two days if you want to. You can come by the house and get the horse when you need him."

"Thank you, Sheriff. I'll get an early start on the grave tomorrow morning. I think the weather is going to be good for the rest of the week."

Bob got up early the next morning, ate a quick breakfast at the Café, and soon went on his way to the graveyard at the Baptist Church. With a mattock he carefully made an outline on the ground the size of the grave he was going to dig for Sally's second burial.

"Sure hope I don't dig into any rock," Bob said as he began to dig into the soft mountain dirt.

It was after dinner time, and Bob hadn't slowed down with his digging. He was lucky that he didn't have to dig through any rock and the grave was deep enough. All he needed to do now was smooth the sides, and he would be finished.

He located some old lumber to cover the hole so that no one or any animals would fall in the hole before he put Sally in it. After Sally was in the grave he would fill it with the dirt that was in a pile beside the grave. He was proud of the neat hole he had dug.

He left the church cemetery and went straight to the funeral home to put his digging tools on the sled. He would need them tomorrow when he made the trip up the mountain to dig Sally up and bring her back to the church for a decent burial.

It was late in the evening when he arrived back at the jail. He was tired and ready to wash-up and call it a day.

"I'm only half done with this job," Bob said as he was getting into his bed. "I didn't know that it would cause all this much work and trouble when I killed her. Wish I had just left and never gone back."

Bob didn't sleep too well that night. He was wide awake thinking of what Sally would look like when he dug her up. It had been quite a while since he buried her out near the barn at their home on the mountainside. When he finally dozed off, he began to have bad dreams. He sat straight up in bed looking all around. He had been dreaming that Sally was lying on the floor all wrapped up in the oil cloth that came from his kitchen table.

"I guess I wrapped her up after I shot her. I don't remember much after she hit me in the head with that iron skillet. Things sort of went black for a few minutes. I don't remember much about carrying her to the barn or digging the grave, either. I was still real dizzy when the Sheriff came to visit. He didn't get to see her because I had the grave filled and was piling mountain rocks on it.

I didn't want any wild animals digging her up."

Bob was the only customer in the Café where he was eating his breakfast the next morning.

"Yore up awful early. Hit's usually around eight when you come for breakfast. Something special happening today?" The cook at the Café was trying to get Bob to tell him what he was up to, but Bob never gave him an answer. He just kept eating at a fast pace.

Bob left the Café and went to the funeral home. He started to ring the door bell when he noticed a sign on the wall. "Office Hours 9 AM to 5 PM -- Call HW59-9292 for Emergencies." He left the funeral home and headed toward the Sheriff's house.

"I'll get the horse and come back for the sled and coffin".

Bob was anxious to get started with moving Sally from her mountain grave to the new one at the Baptist Church. When he arrived at the Sheriff's house, there were no lights on in the house. This told him that everyone was still sleeping. He went to the barn to get the horse. The horse was in its stall, but it had not been fed. Bob went to the corn crib and brought six ears of corn back for the horse. He knew that no one ever worked their horses without feeding them first. He located the harness and a singletree. He hadn't noticed if the sled he was borrowing from the funeral home had a singletree. He would take it along just in case there wasn't one on the sled.

As he stepped out of the tack room into the hallway, he saw the Sheriff coming down the trail toward the barn.

"Good morning, Bob. Up and about real early. Must

be a big day ahead for you. I've come to feed the horse."

"I've done fed him. I gave him six ears of corn. It'll be dinner time before I ever get started digging Sally up. The funeral home don't open 'til nine, and it'll take at least an hour to get there. I sure will be glad when this job is finished. I didn't know it would be this much trouble."

"See you this evening," the Sheriff said as he left to go back to his house.

Bob was at the funeral home when the owner came to open for business.

"Come to borrow the sled and pick up the casket. Got to get on my way. Lots of work to get done before dark. I'll get the horse hooked to the sled and pull around back so we can load the casket. Shore wish I had never started this. Lots of trouble for nothing."

It was around eleven o'clock when Bob stopped the horse beside the spot where he had buried Sally a little over a year ago. The grass and weeds had grown up around the grave, but all the rocks he had put on the grave were still there.

Bob unhitched the horse from the sled and took him to the barn. He returned and began to remove the rocks from the grave.

"Sure hope I don't find any snakes. Nothing in this world more dangerous than a big mountain rattler. If one bit me I would be dead before I could get off this mountain. Yes sir, they shore are mean."

The rocks were soon off the grave, and Bob was digging and shoveling as fast as he could. He soon had the dirt removed enough to be able to see the oil cloth that Sally was wrapped in. He quit using the shovel and started moving the dirt with his hands.

"Got to be careful and not let her get out of the wrapper. Sure would be a mess trying to pick her up in little pieces".

Soon all the dirt was off, and Bob got out of the hole and sat on the rock pile.

"Wonder what Sally looks like?" Curiosity was getting the best of Bob.

"Think I'll take a little peek."

He got back in the grave, untied one end of the cloth she was wrapped in, carefully opened it, and jumped out of the hole. What he saw was not Sally. She had red hair, and the hair Bob saw was blue or black. He didn't stay in the hole long enough to really know what it was.

Bob finally got calm enough to see that the bones and hair he had seen were not those of a human.

"Got to go get the Sheriff. He will know what to do."

Down the sled road he went. He would walk fast for a while, and then run until he was out of breath. When he arrived at the jail, the Sheriff was sitting behind his desk. He had his eyes shut and was taking a little nap.

"Sheriff! Sheriff!" Bob hollered. "You got to come with me and see what's in the grave where Sally was supposed to be. You won't believe what is in that grave."

"Slow down. Slow down. I can't understand anything you are saying."

"Come on, Sheriff. You will not believe what you see."

The Sheriff got up and walked toward the door where Bob was standing.

"We'll take the car to the foot of the mountain. Be faster than walking."

The Sheriff parked the Ford on the side of the road at

the foot of the mountain were the sled road began. Bob was out of the car before the Sheriff could get his door open.

"Come on, Sheriff. Better hurry before some wild animal gets in the grave and eats Sally or whatever is rolled up in that oil cloth."

Bob was at least twenty feet in front of the Sheriff all the way up the mountain. He was standing by the hole where the corpse lay when the Sheriff staggered up and said, "I'll have to get my breath back before I get in that hole and have a look at whatever you buried over a year ago."

He slowly lowered himself down to where the oil cloth was wrapped around what was supposed to be the body of Sally, Bob's dead wife. He untied the twine that was around the wrapping, opened it and said, "Bob, you buried a big dog instead of your wife Sally. There is blue and white hair and a skeleton of a dog all wrapped up."

"That's Ol' Blue, my possum and coon dog. I was wondering what went with him while I was in jail. Thought that he may have gone over to the Henson's house. They have two or three dogs, and Ol' Blue went over there every once and a while."

"Well, what are you going to do?" he asked Bob.

"If you will help me put ever what is wrapped in that oil cloth in the coffin, I'll take it to the Baptist Church and bury it in the grave I dug for Sally. Don't want to have done all that digging for nothing. And besides, Ol' Blue was a lots better to me than Sally was."

The Sheriff helped Bob get the skeleton in the coffin on the sled, and he started to leave.

"See you tomorrow morning. Be sure and feed the

horse when you take him home."

After Bob filled the hole and hitched the horse to the sled, he headed down the mountain toward the church graveyard. All the way to the graveyard he was trying to think back to what happened that day he thought he killed Sally for hitting him in the head with that iron frying pan. "Got to get this mess figured out," he thought.

THE INVESTIGATION

The Sheriff was late coming to work the next morning. Bob had already opened the office and was waiting for him.

"Morning, Sheriff. Did you figure out why Ol' Blue was in the grave instead of Sally? Didn't sleep a wink last night trying to figure out what happened. Sure would like to know how things got mixed up like they did. Sure hate that Ol' Blue got killed. Best tree dog in the county. When you heard him let out his tree bark, you could bet your bottom dollar he had a big coon or possum up a tree."

"I didn't sleep well myself," said the Sheriff. I feel like I didn't do my duty that day I came to your house and you told me you had killed your wife. I should have checked to see what you were burying and ordered you to have a decent funeral. Yes, sir, I sure messed up. Going to take some time to figure this thing out. Best that we don't tell anybody about this. We both might get run out of the county."

"You can count on me, Sheriff. No one will ever hear anything from me. I'm a free man. I served my sentence for killing Sally, and the case is closed. But I would still like to know what went with Sally."

"Think you can handle things around here for a couple of weeks? I have some vacation time due, and I think I will take it and solve this mix-up once and for all."

"Sure can," said Bob. "Everything is pretty quiet around here since the Revenuers left. A fight or someone who drank too much moonshine is about all that has happened lately. Hate to see you use your vacation time trying to find Sally. Even if you do find her, I don't want her coming back. Wish I had never married her in the first place."

"Where was the place that you found Sally? Got to have some place to start solving this mystery."

"One of the boys down at the feed store told me about her. Said she lived over in Haysville. That's a little town over the mountain near that big lake that's in North Carolina and Georgia. Lots of fishermen from both states fish that lake. All kinds of fish in it, even some trout."

"Never been fishing, but I'm about to take up the sport. I'll borrow some fishing stuff from Ray Wise. He does a lot of fishing. Goes about every time he is off from his job at the tannery. Don't want anyone to know that I am a lawman when I start nosing around Haysville. What was Sally's family name? You told me, but I forgot it."

"Ensley. Sally Ensley before we were married. Big family. Mom and dad real friendly. Don't know why Sally turned out so mean. Should have took one of the older girls for a wife. Been lots better to have married one who was not as pretty. Maybe she would have let me live in the same house with her. Shore made a big mistake when I picked Sally for my wife."

"Better help me find a way to cover the 'Sheriff' sign on the door of my car. I don't want anyone to know that I'm a lawman. When I talk to the people around Haysville, I want them to think I'm just another fisherman who's come to fish in that big lake they have over there. If they know that I'm a lawman, they will shy away from me, and I'll never get this case closed."

Early the next morning when the Sheriff arrived at the jail Bob was sweeping the floor. He quit, stood scratching his head, squinted his eyes, and said, "Is that you, Sheriff?"

The Sheriff looked at Bob with a big grin on his face. "Yep, it's me".

He didn't look like himself. He was wearing a pair of bibbed overalls, a blue denim shirt, and a felt hat that looked like someone had sat on it. There were fishing lures stuck all over the hat.

"Think I'll pass for a fisherman?" he asked.

"Don't know what a fisherman looks like, never been fishing in my whole life," Bob said. "Makes no difference. Guess them people who live over there have seen all kinds of fishermen. You look all right to me. Don't matter if you catch any fish or not. You're going to try and catch Sally if she is still alive."

The Sheriff in his new role of "fisherman" left the jail and was on his way to Haysville. Fishing was not on his mind. All he could think about was how to locate Bob's "dead" wife and solve the mystery of Ol' Blue being in the grave instead of Sally who Bob thought he killed and buried near the barn at his home on the mountain. He worried about why he had not investigated the murder. That was a part of his job as Sheriff. If he had done his duty as Sheriff, Ol' Bob wouldn't have served a year in jail for killing Sally. Everything about this murder was a big mystery, and he intended to solve it.

An hour had gone by when the door to the office opened and the Sheriff headed to his desk.

"What's the problem, Sheriff?" Bob asked.

"Forgot my Sheriff's badge. I may need to show it. Never can tell."

"Better take your gun, too," Bob said. All the people over at the lake may be as mean as Sally, and you may need it."

The Sheriff opened the drawer of his desk and picked up the pistol that he sometimes carried while on duty.

"I'm taking the bullets out. I'll have to carry it in my front pocket. If it should accidentally fire, it would blow my leg off."

"Good idea," said Bob.

"Better get going. I'm late already. It's bad luck to come back after starting somewhere." The Sheriff was talking to himself as he left the office.

"See you in a day or two, maybe sooner if I find out what happened to Sally." He was still talking when the door closed.

He was soon on the narrow, paved road going to Haysville. The speedometer read 30 miles per hour. This was as fast as he ever drove the A-model. He had the side windows turned so the cool air filled the car. He was comfortable but not relaxed. A million thoughts were going through his head about what he would do if he should find Sally. What would he do if she refused to tell him what happened?

He pulled the Ford to the side of the road and turned the ignition switch off. He looked up and down the road to see if anyone was around. He opened the door, got out, and went to the back of the car. The trunk wasn't locked. He opened it, reached in, and brought out a half-gallon fruit jar filled with what looked like clear water. The Sheriff was known to always keep a jar of moonshine in the car just in case someone got sick and needed a little medicine. He removed the lid and put the jar to his mouth. After three or four swallows he smacked his lips and said, "Ahh. Mighty good stuff. I needed that to steady my nerves."

After a couple of more rest stops and a little more refreshment, the Sheriff noticed that he was nearing the town of Haysville. There were houses on both sides of the road. Children were playing in some of the yards. On his right he noticed a large "Nehi" sign.

"Must be a store. I'll stop and ask about where I can find the Ensley house."

He was getting really nervous but didn't dare go to the jar in the back of the car. He was afraid the Ensleys would smell the moonshine and think he was just a drunk who had lost his way home. "Got to have a clear mind and find Bob's girl Sally," he thought.

He parked the car in front of the store, got out, and walked toward the entrance. As he stepped on the porch of the store, the door opened, and a young man who looked like he was around twenty years old came out.

"Pardon me," the Sheriff said. "Can you tell me

where the Ensley family lives?"

"What's the man's given name?" he asked. "There are two Ensley families on this side of the lake."

"Don't know what they call him. All I know is, there are several girls in the family."

"Oh. That has to be Big John. He's a big feller. Must weigh over two-hundred fifty. Don't do a whole lot of work. Just enough to feed that bunch of girls he has. Bet he wishes he could get them married off. Then he could retire for sure."

"That must be the one I'm looking for. Where is his house?"

"Go down the road toward the lake. When you come to the second road on your right, take a turn. His house is the first one you come to on the right. A big white house with a porch all the way across the front. He'll probably be sitting in his rocking chair on the porch. He likes to look out over the lake."

"Thanks. I'd better get going. Be dark pretty soon, and I don't know my way around Haysville. First time I've been here."

The Sheriff started the engine of the Ford and backed out of the parking lot. A thousand things were running through his mind:

"What will I say when I meet John Ensley? How will I get to meet the girls? How will I know if one of the girls is Sally? Will she talk with me if I do find her?"

The closer he got to where Big John lived, the more nervous he got. Sweat began to pop out on his forehead. "Better calm down," the Sheriff said to himself. "Don't want to give myself away."

He pulled the Ford into the driveway of the house

and got out. On the porch was a very big man sitting in a rocking chair. His hair was uncombed and was showing some graying. Also, it looked as if he hadn't shaved for several days.

"Howdy, stranger. Grab a chair and set a spell," Big John said. "You're new around here. What brings you to Haysville?"

"Yep. It's my first time here. I live up in Haywood County. I heard that the fishing was pretty good in this lake you have down here. A friend told me to look you up if I ever decided to do some fishing here. Said you knew more about this lake than anyone around. Said you would tell me where the best spot was to catch some of them big crappy that're in this lake."

"I don't like to brag, but I guess I've caught more fish out of this lake than any two fishermen. Yep. I've been fishing here since I was knee-high -- around fifty years, I guess. It's no use wandering all over the lake looking for the best fishing hole. See that big willow just up to your right? Now no one likes that spot because they are always hanging their line in that tree. All you have to do is sort'a drop your line a little ways out, and you'll drag in the biggest crappie in the whole country. I'd appreciate it if you wouldn't let the word out about this."

"It's getting pretty late in the day. I guess I'll find me a place to sleep and get an early start tomorrow."

"Good Idea," Big John said. There's a motel about a mile down the road. It's not a fancy place, but it's clean and pretty cheap. About all the business they get is from people who come down here to fish. They have a restaurant in the lobby where you can get a pretty good breakfast. About all you can get there the rest of the day is some kind of sandwich."

"Well, I'd better get going. It'll soon be dark. Thanks for telling me where to fish. I'll stop by before I leave and let you know how many fish I caught."

As the Sheriff was leaving the porch, he happened to look toward the open door. There was a young girl peeping out, and she had bright red hair.

"This has to be the right family, and from the way Bob described Sally, this has to be her. It won't take long to get this thing straightened out," he said to himself. "I'll do my fishing and come back tomorrow."

The Sheriff didn't sleep too well that night. He lay awake thinking how he could get a good look at the red-headed girl he had seen through the front door as he left the Ensley house.

"I wish I had brought another jar of nerve medicine. I need something to calm me down so I can get some sleep."

He was up at dawn the next morning. He washed his face and got dressed in the fishing clothes he had brought along. After taking all of his stuff to the car, he went to the snack bar at the front of the motel. He sat on a stool at the counter and picked up a menu. There wasn't a lot to choose from. There were eggs any way you wanted them with side orders of bacon, sausage, grits and fried potatoes. Jelly was free of charge with all the meals.

"I'll have two eggs over light, bacon, grits, and a cup of coffee," he said to the girl behind the counter.

"How you want your coffee?" she asked.

"Black," the Sheriff said.

"Where you from?" the girl asked.

"Haywood County. Come down here to do a little

fishing."

"You won't catch any. The signs are all wrong," she said.

Sheriff Harbin finished eating, paid the waitress, and went to his car. He was soon on his way to the fishing spot that Mr. Ensley had told him about. He turned off the highway and parked the Ford near the lake where it could be seen from the Ensley house. He thought it was possible that he may see the Ensley girls and maybe he could get a good look at the red-headed one. He was more interested in finding Bob's wife than he was in catching fish. He didn't know anything about fishing, anyway. Fishing was only a cover for snooping around to solve the murder of Bob's wife.

To Sheriff Harbin it seemed like a week since he had put his fishing line in the water. He looked at his watch saw that it was 11:25.

"I think I'll quit and go visit the Ensleys again," he said.

He gathered all his fishing equipment and was leaving when he saw a young boy about ten or twelve years old coming out from under the other side of the willow tree.

"Want to buy some fish, Mister?" the boy said.

"I don't think so," the Sheriff said.

He started walking away and then he suddenly stopped. He had an idea. He turned around as the boy was leaving and saw that he had several fish on a stringer.

"How much you want for your fish?" he asked the boy.

"I've got ten nice crappie on this stringer. I'll let you

have 'em all for fifty cents. And you can have the stringer, too."

The Sheriff gave the young boy fifty cents. The boy took a good look at the two quarters and handed the fish to the Sheriff.

"Don't you tell anyone that I bought these fish from you. I want everyone to think I caught them."

"OK, Mister. I won't tell anyone about our deal."

The boy disappeared before the Sheriff could say anything more to him.

The Sheriff put the fish and his fishing pole in his car and drove toward the Ensley's house.

"That has to be Sarah," he said to himself. "I've got to talk with her and get back to Haywood County. Bob may need me."

He pulled into the driveway at the Ensley house and got out of the car. He had the string of fish in his hand and walked toward the house. Big John Ensley was still sitting in his rocking chair on the porch.

"Looks like you had pretty good luck," said Big John.

"I did pretty good. It's awful hot down there by the lake. Do you want a mess of fish?" he asked Big John. "I can't take them back with me. They'd spoil before I got back to Haywood County."

"Don't you like fish?" Big John asked.

"I sure do. There's nothing better than a mess of fresh fish."

"It's still early in the day," Big John said. "Get a chair, and I'll have the girls clean and cook those fish, and you can eat dinner with us before you leave for home."

Sheriff Harbin's plan when buying the fish was to use them as an excuse to get into the Ensley house and find

Sarah. This is what he needed to get a good look at that red-headed girl he saw earlier.

"I don't want to be a lot of trouble to you, but I do like a good mess of fresh fish. I guess I'll take you up on the offer."

"No trouble at all. My girls are real good cooks, and they don't mind company every once and awhile.

"Sally!" Big John yelled. "Come here and get these fish and fix 'em for dinner. We are having company. Hurry it up so he can get on the road before dark."

The red-haired girl came out on the porch to get the fish. She took the fish from the Sheriff and gave him a good look before going back into the house.

"That is Sally as shore as I'm born," the Sheriff said to himself.

"How many girls do you have?" asked the Sheriff.

"Three. That was Sally. She's the youngest."

"How do you keep them from running off and getting married?"

"Only one of them ever married. That's Sally, the one who came for the fish. She run off and married a feller up in Haywood County. It didn't last long, though. She got tired of being married, so she packed up and came back home. You being from Haywood, you may know the man who she was married to. I think his name was Boyd, Bob Boyd."

The Sheriff scratched his head, acting like he was thinking, but he didn't say anything.

One of the other girls came out and said that dinner was ready if they were ready to eat.

Big John didn't waste any time going to the dining room. This was the first time the Sheriff had seen Big

John out of his rocking chair.

No one started eating until everyone was seated at the table. There was a big dish of fried fish, a plate of hush-puppies, cold slaw, and iced tea. It was a meal fit for a king.

Everyone held hands and Mr. Ensley said a short prayer blessing the food. Then everyone began eating. The only one not eating like she was enjoying her meal was the girl with the red hair, Sarah. She kept staring at the Sheriff as if she was trying to figure out where she had seen him.

There was not a lot of talking. About the only talking was someone asking to pass the food. When everyone had finished eating, John and the Sheriff returned to their chairs on the porch.

"Mr. Ensley, I don't want to make you mad or I don't want you to think badly of me, but I need to tell you something. After that fine fish dinner it's even more difficult for me to say what I have to say. I hope you will understand my problem."

"Go ahead and speak your piece. You seem like a fair and honest man."

"You asked me if I know Bob Boyd. I do know him, and he is the reason I came to see you. I didn't want to come down here and start asking questions until I found the person I was looking for. I let on like I was a fisherman so I could look around. I had never fished in my whole life until today. My name is Paul Harbin. I am the Sheriff of Haywood County."

"Did you find what you were looking for?"

"Yes. It's your daughter Sally. I need to talk with her."

"Is she in some kind of trouble?"

"No. I only want to know what happened just before she came back here. When Sally disappeared, Bob thought that he had killed her. He turned himself in at the jail and said he killed Sally. There was a trial, and he was sentenced to prison for a year. After digging up what he thought was Sally's body and discovering that it was not her, he asked me to find out what happened so he could clear his record of being a murderer.

"Sally! Come here. We need to talk with you."

Sally came out on the porch and asked, "What do you want to talk about?"

"This is the Sheriff from Haywood County, and he needs to ask you some questions."

"I thought I had seen him somewhere before," Sally said. "I don't want to talk with him if it's about Bob."

"That's what it's about."

"I ain't talking," said Sally.

"Yes you are," said her Dad.

"Just start at the beginning and tell me what happened that made you decide to come back home all of a sudden."

"Well, on that day Bob was up on the top of the mountain working in the corn field. I was cooking dinner. I was cooking some squirrel that Bob killed that morning. It was frying on the stove, and the smell brought Ol' Blue, Bob's hunting dog, into the house. Now me and that dog never did like each other. I hit him with a broom when I run him out of the house once.

"He came into the kitchen, and when I told him to get out, he growled and showed his teeth. I was afraid he would bite me, so I reached on the wall and got Bob's shotgun. Ol' Blue started toward me, and I shot him.

"I knew that Bob would be coming to the house to find out what I was shooting at, and when he saw what I had done to his dog I would be in big trouble. I took the oil cloth off the eating table, wrapped Ol' Blue up real good, and tied the wrapping real good with string.

"When Bob came in the front door, I was hiding inside, and I hit him real hard with a skillet. He fell over like he was dead. I was scared, so I gathered all my belongings up, put them in a sack, and headed out for home. I stayed in the woods until I was out of town. I didn't want anybody seeing me. A little ways out of town a feller in a truck stopped and gave me a ride all the way to Haysville.

"That's the truth." Is Bob still living?"

"Yes. Bob works for me now. He buried Ol' Blue thinking it was you. I guess he was a little addled from the lick you gave him with that frying pan."

"Thank you for the good meal and telling me what happened between you and Bob," he said to Sally. "I'd better get going if I expect to get home before dark."

"Goodbye, Sally. Goodbye, John."

It was after dark when the Sheriff arrived at the jail in Waynesville. He didn't see any lights on in his office, and he didn't stop.

"I'll not bother Bob tonight. He's probably gone to bed. I'll see him tomorrow. I'd better get on home and go to bed. I need to get a good night's sleep. I didn't sleep much last night at the motel."

The Sheriff turned at the next street and went on his way home.

THE BLUEBIRD GANG

The next morning the Sheriff arrived at the jail and found Bob still in bed. When the Sheriff spoke to him, he jumped out of bed, rubbing his eyes and said to his boss, "When did you get back?"

"Sometime after dark. I don't know what time it was. I didn't see any lights here, so I went straight home. I was real tired from that trip and all the planning about how to locate Sally. Do you want to hear about what I found out?" asked the Sheriff.

"I sure do," said Bob.

"Well, like I said I had to think of a plan to be sure I found the right Sally, the one who you thought you'd killed and buried out near your barn up on the mountain."

The Sheriff went into all the details about how he bought the fish to get to see Sally and question her about what went on the day she disappeared.

"I'm glad you didn't bring her back," Bob said. "I wish she hadn't killed Ol' Blue. He was the best hunting dog I ever owned. Jack Ledbetter over on Beaverdam gave him to me when he was a little pup. He was the runt of the litter. I'd sure like to find another dog as good as he was."

"You'd better bring me up-to-date on all that happened while I was gone," the Sheriff said.

"Everything went real well. We only had one visitor the whole time you were gone. A feller came by and said he was a detective for Southern Railways. He wanted to know if I had heard anything about some boys who were called the 'Bluebird Gang'. I said I had never heard of them. I asked where they were from and why they had that name. He told me they were from around here and that they were stealing from the freight cars on the train that comes through here every day. He didn't know where they got that name, 'Bluebird.'"

"I guess I'd better mosey over to the train station and have a talk with them there. I don't want to let gangs get started in Haywood County. They have them up north, and the police are having a rough time trying to stop all the things they are doing. I hear that it is one more mess in the big northern cities. You hang around until I get back, and we'll talk about what we can do to catch that bunch of 'bluebirds' or at least run them out of the county."

While the Sheriff was gone, Bob made a pot of coffee, straightened up the covers on his bed, and swept the floor. He was hungry but decided to wait until the Sheriff came back and, they could go to the Café on Main Street. That was where Bob ate most of his meals since he started working at the jail. This was also where they got meals for the prisoners when they had any. The people they locked up were usually arrested for being drunk or for fighting. They only stayed over-night and were released before breakfast. This saved the county tax money.

It was nearly lunch time when the Sheriff returned to the jail.

"I glad you're back," said Bob. I've nearly starved to death. I ain't eaten anything since about five-thirty yesterday. I hope the Café is still serving breakfast."

"I don't know how they ever run a train and get there on schedule. They're the slowest people I ever saw. They didn't come to work until nine o'clock. Then they took a break for coffee. They sure run a loose business. I finally got to talk with the feller who's in charge of the train station. I didn't get a whole lot of information out of him. He said that the Southern detectives were working on the case but would appreciate any help I could give them.

"Well, Bob, I guess it's up to you and me to break up or catch the Bluebird Gang. All the railroad men told me was that the thieves were opening up boxcars that had candy, cigarettes, and small stuff that they could sell real cheap. They didn't know how many were in the gang, how old they were, or where they lived. In fact, all they seemed to know was that someone was stealing from them, and they had to pay for the losses."

"What are we going to do?" Bob asked.

"I don't know right off. I'll think of something," Sheriff Harbin said.

Bob and the Sheriff both looked at each other. Neither one said anything. They were both trying to think of a way to get started on the Bluebird Gang case.

"It won't be easy," said the Sheriff. "But I think I have

a plan to get started on the case."

"What do you have in mind?" Bob asked excitedly.

"Well, I was thinking that one of us would have to get close to someone in the gang and find out how they operate. Once we find out when they are planning on robbing the train, we can set a trap and catch them."

"I don't think I could be the undercover man. It seems everyone knows me or has heard of me. I doubt if they know you, and if they did, they would have heard about your killing Sally. Your reputation as a bad guy might help you get to know them and get accepted into their gang. It could be dangerous, and if you don't want to take the chance, I'll not order you to do it."

"I'll take the chance," Bob said. "I've never been afraid of any man or animal. I can take care of 'Bob'. When do you want me to start the investigation?"

"You'd better change your clothes. They'll get suspicious seeing you in that outfit. And you can't take your gun. I'll come up with a plan by tomorrow, and you can get started. I'll have to get permission from the County Commission for you to have an expense account. You can't be seen here in Waynesville, so you will have to stay in Canton and eat at the Café there. You may have to buy some of the stolen items for evidence."

"Bob was really excited about being on his own and trying to solve a crime. If he caught the members of the Bluebird Gang, maybe he would get the Deputy's job full-time and the local people would forget about his trial and his jail term for killing Sally. They didn't know what the Sheriff had found out about Sally and that she confessed to what she did to make it look like he killed her."

"Get a good night's sleep," the Sheriff said. "You may

have to walk all the way to Canton. I can't take you because some of the gang might see us together, and our plans would be spoiled. They would know that you were working for me. Maybe someone will pick you up. They're not many cars on old Route 19-23 these days. Gas is nearly fifteen cents a gallon, so people who have a car drive only when they have to. They want to save their gas."

"It's only about twelve miles from Waynesville to Canton. I'll be there before dinner if I leave around seven in the morning," Bob said. "I'll get up around six and eat breakfast at the Café. It stays open twenty-four hours a day, and not many people eat that early. Tonight I'll get a few things together that I might need. I probably won't take my shaving stuff. I'll grow a beard, and if I should bump into someone who knows me, they wouldn't recognize who I am. I guess one of them big paper pokes from the grocery store will hold all I'll need."

"It seems to me like you got everything planned out," the Sheriff said.

Sheriff Harbin gathered all of the papers on his desk and put them in the desk drawer. As he was putting the papers away he said to Bob, "If I don't see you tomorrow morning before you leave for Canton, I'll tell you once more: Don't take any chances of getting hurt. If things get out of hand or if you think they have figured out who you are working for, pack up and come back to Waynesville. You have made me a very good Deputy, and I don't want to lose you."

"Don't worry, Sheriff. I think everything will work out fine and we will have the Bluebird Gang in jail before you know it. That is, some of them if not the whole gang.

Go on home and get a good night's sleep. Don't worry about old Bob."

Before going to bed Bob got all the things he was taking with him and put them in a big paper bag. All he would have to do tomorrow morning would be eat breakfast at the Café and head out toward Canton. He didn't mind walking those twelve miles. He had walked them on several occasions before. And he may get lucky and get a ride from one of the pulpwood trucks that carry chestnut or pine wood to the paper mill at Canton.

Bob didn't sleep too well that night. He lay awake thinking about all the things that could happen -- some good, some bad. He was also thinking about where he could find a place to sleep in Canton. He had lived alone in his log house up in the mountains, and he knew how to take care of himself. Even after marrying Sally, he had to fend for himself.

Bob was out of bed by five o'clock the next morning. He washed up and dressed in the clothes he was wearing when he came to the jail. He didn't take the bag he had packed when he went to eat breakfast. He didn't want anyone asking why he had the bag and where was he going. No one but the Sheriff and Bob knew about their plan to catch the Bluebird Gang or at least break up the gang and stop their stealing from the Southern Railway boxcars.

Bob was walking alongside of Highway 19-23 on his way to Canton when about three miles out of Waynesville a pick-up truck passed and stopped a short distance in front of him.

"Want a ride young feller?" the driver asked.

"I'm not tired, but a ride would be fine. It's about

nine more miles to Canton. I hope that's where you are headed."

"I'm going right through Canton on my way to Asheville," he said to Bob. "I'd be glad to give you a lift. It'll be lots faster than walking."

"Yep, sure will."

Bob had been told by the Sheriff not to talk to anyone about where he was from and why he was going to Canton. In fact, the Sheriff had said, "Be as quiet as you can."

Sure enough, the driver started asking questions.

"Where are you from?" he asked.

"I've lived all my life up on the mountain above Waynesville," said Bob.

"What are you going to Canton for?" the driver asked.

"I'm looking for a job," Bob said.

"Aren't there any jobs around Waynesville?" the driver asked.

"Nope. I don't make enough to live on by working my place on the mountain and doing a little farm work for my neighbors ever now and then. They only pay ten cents an hour plus dinner."

"Are you married?" he asked.

"Nope. I'm thinking about marrying if I can get a job that pays enough to keep up a woman. I talked to some of my buddies who got married, and they told me a woman would spend every dime you could make. They're always needing something."

"Are you married?" Bob asked the driver.

"Yep. Been married nearly ten years. My old lady doesn't care a lot about buying everything she sees when she goes to town. I've got a mighty fine woman. She takes care of me real well. Not many men can say that about their wives."

"I sure hope I can find one like that. How can I find out if someone will make a good wife? It will be too late after you're married if she turns out bad."

"Well, when you find the girl you think you love, don't rush into getting married. Hang around her house as much as you can and watch her mama real close. The way she works and how she treats her husband is usually how her daughter will be. The old saying, 'Like mama, like daughter', is usually true."

"Thank you for the advice. I'll remember that," Bob said.

The question and answer session ended, and both men were quiet for the rest of the trip.

There were soon lots of houses along the road as they came closer to the town of Canton.

"We're getting close to town," the driver said.

"Where do you want me to stop in town?"

"Anywhere it's easy for you," Bob said. "I guess this is as good a place as any. I've never been to Canton before today."

The driver pulled his old truck to the curb in front of the Colonel Theater.

"Good luck with the job hunting. I hope you find a good one so you can get married and settle down," the driver said.

"Thanks for the ride. I've got over a half day to look around for a place to live while I'm here looking for a job."

The truck drove away, and Bob stood on the sidewalk

looking first up the street and then down. He was trying to decide which way he would go. He finally decided
to look for a café. He could get a bite to eat and also
talk with the waiter about where he could find a place to
board.

It was past the dinner time, and there were only two
customers in the café when Bob entered. He went to a
table off in the corner away from the two men who were
eating at the counter. He didn't want anyone to hear him
asking the waiter about Canton.

The waiter brought a drinking glass and a picture of
water to the table where Bob was sitting.

"What will it be, young feller?" the waiter asked.

"Could I see a menu of what you have for dinner?"
Bob asked.

"Sure. Coming right up."

The waiter left, went behind the counter, got a menu,
and returned to the table where Bob was sitting. He
handed the menu to Bob and said, "Take your time, and
when you decide what you want, give me a holler." He
then left Bob and returned to the kitchen.

Bob looked over the menu to see what they had that
he liked. He didn't worry about what it would cost because he was spending the County Commission's money.
He didn't give any thought to the fact that it was money
that came out of his own taxes.

Bob began to go down the list on the menu: "beef
stew, hamburger steak with fries, chicken and dumplings...." These were the main dishes. The menu also
listed "mashed potatoes, green beans, sweet potatoes, and
turnip greens". The desserts were "apple cobbler, choco-
late pie, and jelled fruit salad". On the back of the menu

there was a list of about any kind of sandwich you could think of. They even had "hotdogs with chili".

Bob had trouble deciding what he wanted to eat. Everything looked good to him. The Café in Waynesville where he ate most of his meals didn't' have all these choices.

The waiter came to the table where Bob was sitting and said, "Have you decided what you want for dinner?"

"It all looks good, but I think I'll have the beef stew, sweet potatoes, and green beans."

"Corn bread or rolls?" .

"Rolls. And some butter."

"And your drink?"

"Do you have a Nehi 'orange'?"

"Sure do."

"That's what I'll have," Bob said.

"Be back in a jiffy."

The waiter was gone before Bob could ask him about where he could rent a room in Canton.

When Bob's food was brought to his table he thanked the waiter and didn't ask him any questions. He decided to wait until he had finished eating.

When the waiter came back to Bob's table, Bob noticed that all the customers were gone except him. This was the time to ask about a place to rent.

"Do you know where I can rent a room?" Bob asked.

"There're only two places I know of. One is the Hotel and the other is the rooms above the Hipps Grocery Store. The Hotel always has empty rooms, but I don't know about the Hipps place. I'll call them and ask if you want me to."

"I sure would appreciate it if you would. If you ask,

they may have a vacancy. If I asked them, they may be a little scared to take in a stranger. Mighty nice of you to do this for me."

The waiter went to the counter, picked up the telephone, and dialed. Bob couldn't hear what he was saying, so he sat still and waited.

"You're lucky. They have a room. I told them to hold it for you. I didn't know what name to give them, but I told the manager you were a clean-looking young man. Go into the grocery store, ask for Mr. Hipps, and he will tell you all about the cost and other things."

"How do I find the Hipps Building?" Bob asked.

"When you leave here, turn right, go to the first red light, and turn left. After you cross the railroad tracks, keep going until you reach another red light. Turn left and keep going to another red light. You'll see a grocery store, and that's the Hipps Building. Do you think you can find it," the waiter asked.

"Shouldn't be any problem," Bob said.

Bob went to the cash register on the counter and asked, "How much do I owe you for the dinner?"

The waiter began to punch the buttons on the cash register. Bells were pinging, and Bob thought about what the dinner would cost. "It must be a lot from the sound of that machine."

"You owe me a total of seventy-five cents. It usually costs about fifty-cents for dinner, but you ate a lot more than most of my customers. You must not have eaten breakfast."

"The Café in Waynesville where I usually eat doesn't have much on its menu. Why do you have all these choices?"

"Monday through Friday, between 12:00 and 13:00, this place is packed. The workers from the paper mill come here for dinner. It sure beats the lunch that their old ladies pack, most of them say. I try to have something cooked that they will like. Lots of them eat the beef stew and others like the chicken and dumplings. If they find what they like, they come back."

Bob paid for his dinner and thanked the waiter again for the good meal and for finding him a place to stay. He left the Café and went on his way to find the Hipps Building.

Bob didn't have any trouble locating the store. He went in and asked for Mr. Hipps. An elderly man, probably in his fifties, came over to Bob and said, "You must be the boy that the Café called about."

"Yes sir. My name is Bob Boyd. I live on the mountain at Waynesville. I'm looking for a job. When I find steady work, I'm thinking about getting married. That is, if I can find a woman who will marry me."

"Go back out the front door, turn right, and go up the steps to the second floor. Mrs. Parks is expecting you. She's the manager of the boarding house. In fact, she does everything: the cooking, the cleaning, and the whole thing. She'll tell you all about the cost and the rules that you must follow if you want to live in her boarding house."

Mrs. Parks was waiting at the top of the stairs. She must have been expecting Bob. The Hipps man downstairs must have called her or tipped her off some way or another.

"Are you the young feller looking for a place to sleep?" she asked.

"Yes, mum. I sure am glad I found your place."

"There are a few rules I have that you must follow if you want to stay here. There will be no parties in your room. If you come in late at night, you will be very quiet and not wake the others who are staying here. I will bring clean sheets and clean your room once a week. You can exchange your dirty towels for clean ones every day.

"The cost for the room is fifty-cents a night. You pay in advance for a full week, which is seven-fifty. If you want to eat here, I serve three meals a day, except on Sundays. I serve breakfast and dinner on Sunday, but no supper meal. You pay for the meals you eat here. The cost is fifty-cents for each meal you eat. Do you have any questions?"

"No mum," Bob said.

"Oh, I didn't tell you about the bathroom. There is one at each end of the hall. You can use either one you want to. Both have a tub and a shower. Mind you, don't waste the hot water. Your room is number 13. You're not superstitious, are you?" she asked.

"No mum. I don't believe in 13 being unlucky, but I do believe that black cats are bad luck, and there also are ghosts and 'haints'. And I don't want to break a looking glass. That's seven years bad luck for sure."

"Breakfast is from six to seven every morning; dinner is twelve until one, and supper is five until six-thirty every day except Sunday. There is no supper meal on Sunday."

"Hope you like staying here," Mrs. Parks said as she walked away.

Bob closed the door to his room, took his clothes from the grocery bag, and placed them in the drawer of the wash stand that was in the corner of the room. After looking the room over very closely, he moved the chair over to the window and gave the neighborhood a good looking over. He was a little restless and thinking what his next move would be to find some member of the Bluebird Gang and make friends with him. "Where can I look for them?" Bob asked himself.

Bob went to the bathroom at the end of the hall. He didn't take a bath. He washed his face and hands. "Didn't do anything today to get dirty," Bob said to himself.

"I'll eat supper, get a good night's sleep, and start searching tomorrow. It's too late in the day to begin now. Maybe I'll think of some plan before then."

When Bob went to the dining room for supper, there were several men seated there at a long, wooden dining table. There were chairs for ten people at the table. He sat down by a man who was already eating. The man turned and looked at Bob.

"Have you just moved in?" he asked Bob.

"Yes. About two hours ago."

"Where're you from?" the man asked.

"My name's Bob Boyd. I'm from Waynesville. I thought I might find a job around here. Do you know where there's a good place to find a job?" he asked his new friend.

"I don't think the paper mill is hiring anyone at the present, but the construction contractor at the mill way need another hand. While you are looking around town, don't go to the pool hall or the beer joint down on Main Street. The crowd that hangs out at those places don't want a job, and about all of them have a reputation for being in trouble with the Law. They're a pretty mean bunch. Several have been in prison for stealing and running moonshine."

Bob had heard about just what he was looking for. The pool hall would be his first place to visit tomorrow morning, and then he'd pay a visit to the beer joint.

"I'm sure glad I met this man" Bob thought to himself. "Everything has gone well since I left Waynesville: First the ride, then finding a place to stay, and now information about where to start looking for the Bluebird Gang. I couldn't have planned anything as good as what happened on my first day of the investigation."

After Bob finished eating his supper, he got up from the table, and while he was leaving, he said, "I didn't ask you what your name is.

"Henry -- Henry Haney. I work in the Electrical Department at the paper mill. I've been there for nigh on twenty years. It's a good place to work, and the pay is pretty good. I've been staying at this boarding house for nearly two years now. I come here right after me and my wife got divorced. I'm never going to marry again. I've learned my lesson."

"I'll be seeing you around, Henry," Bob said. "Thanks for all the information you gave me."

Bob got up early the next morning and got ready to start the assignment that the Sheriff had given him. But first, he needed to go to the dining room for breakfast. When he entered the room, he looked for a place to sit. There was someone sitting in all the chairs but one. He made a bee-line for that seat before someone else could beat him to it. He was in a hurry, and he didn't want to be standing around waiting for someone to finish eating and leave.

Bob hurried eating his breakfast and got up from the table to go back to his room.

"What time do the stores and other businesses around here open?" he asked the man who had sat by him at breakfast.

"Some stores open at nine, but most places don't open before ten o'clock," he told Bob.

Bob went to his room. When he looked at the clock sitting on the table beside his bed, she saw that it was seven-thirty, nearly three hours before the pool hall would open.

Bob said to himself, "I Guess I could walk around town and window-shop until ten o'clock. I might bump into someone to talk to. It wouldn't do any harm to go to the Café and have a cup of coffee. There could be someone there I could talk with. I'm sure not sitting in this room for two and a half hours. It'd be kind of like sitting around the jail waiting for something to happen."

Bob had seen what was in the window of every store twice before nine o'clock. The walk around the one block that made up the main part of the town of Canton didn't take a lot of time. He only met a couple of people, and they seemed to be in a hurry.

"They're probably going to work," Bob thought. "I may as well go to the Café and drink coffee until ten."

When he entered the Café, Bob noticed a young man sitting at one of the tables eating. He was younger than Bob. He was probably eighteen years old or there about.

Bob went to the counter and asked for a cup of coffee. The waiter handed him a cup of coffee, and Bob went to the table where the young man was eating breakfast.

"Do you mind if I join you?" Bob asked.

"I don't mind at all. Pull up a chair."

Bob sat down facing the young fellow on the other side of the table.

"I don't know much about Canton. I just got here yesterday," Bob said to the young man.

"Where are you from?" he asked Bob.

"I'm from Waynesville. I've come to Canton looking for a job."

"What's your name?" he asked Bob.

"Robert Boyd. People call me 'Bob.'"

"My name is Brad Hall. I've lived here all my life. Glad to meet you," he said as reached across the table to shake hands with Bob.

"Bob Boyd …. Bob Boyd…. I've heard that name before. I heard my dad talking about you a year or two ago. Bob Boyd…. Yeah. Are you the Bob Boyd who killed his wife a couple of years ago?"

"Guess so. I wouldn't have killed her if she hadn't hit me with an iron skillet. She nearly killed me first," Bob said. "I guess my killing Sally is the reason I can't get a job. Everything is fine when they interview me until they ask if I have a criminal record. When I tell them I was in jail for a year, they stop asking questions. They come from behind their desk, shake hands with me and say, 'If anything comes up, I'll give you a call.' I could lie to them, but I was raised not to ever lie to anyone. Daddy said, 'Son, always tell the truth even if it hurts you.' It sure has hurt, but I'll keep looking for a job."

Brad stopped eating, looked straight at Bob, and said, "Bob, you and me have the same problem. I got caught with a case of moonshine in my car, and I had to serve a year in prison out in Ohio. When I answer that I have a prison record, the job interview ends right there."

"Where do you earn money to buy gas for your car?" Bob asked.

"I'm back in the moonshine business," Brad said. "I can't find a regular job, so I got to work somewhere."

"Ain't that kind of risky?" Bob said.

"Not as risky as the other way I tried to earn a living."

"What were you doing before selling moonshine?" Bob asked.

"Robbing trains," Brad said.

"Robbing trains? You must be kidding," Bob said to Brad.

"Nope. We were robbing trains --Southern Railway freight trains," Brad said.

"Who was 'we'?" Bob asked.

"A Pressley boy from Waynesville -- Paul Pressley -- and another boy from Asheville by the name of Stone, Jim Stone.

Jim was the most important one of our gang. He would watch the train cars being loaded in Asheville at the warehouse and mark which ones we needed to steal from."

"You said something about a gang. What do you mean?"

"Well, we didn't call ourselves a 'gang', and we never had any kind of a name. Word got out from the railroad people that there was a gang robbing certain rail cars as the train went through the Mangus Cut here in Canton. People said we would take what we wanted and fly away like a bunch of bluebirds. Everyone began to refer to us as the 'Blue Bird Gang'."

"Why did you choose the Mangus Cut?" Bob asked Brad.

"The Mangus Cut is a steep hill between two small mountains where the train moves about as fast as a man can walk. We would open the door on the car that Jim had marked before the train left Asheville. One of us would get in the car and hand the cigarettes, candy, or whatever we took to the two walking along beside the train."

"What would you do with the things you took from the train?" Bob asked Brad.

"We tried to sell what we took from the train, but no one wanted to buy it. We were selling cigarettes for fifty cents a carton and a box of candy for a quarter. That was a nickel for a pack of cigarettes and two cents a bar for candy."

"Are you still stealing from the rail cars?" Bob asked.

"No. We quit about a month ago," he said to Bob. "Jim went back to Asheville; Paul and me rented a house and started selling moonshine again. We make pretty good money from boot-legging, but we're taking a big chance of getting caught. I don't know any way to earn a living other than stealing or selling liquor. Like you said, if you have a prison record, no one will give you a job. What are you going to do when you can't find a job here in Canton?"

"I guess I'll go back to Waynesville."

"I'm glad you joined me for breakfast," Brad said. "I was beginning to think that I was the only person in the whole world who had this problem when trying to find an honest job. Do you want to ride out and see where Paul and I live?" Brad asked.

"Sure do. I don't have anything special planned for today," Bob said.

Bob and Brad paid the cashier and left the Café.

"Where's your car?" Bob asked.

Brad pointed to a shinny, model-A Ford coup parked beside the Café. "It's the fastest Ford in Haywood County," Brad said. "I'll put her up against any car around, including the police cars. I had Hugh Wines at the garage on Railroad Street rebuild the engine. I don't know what he did, but I do know that it will go at least twenty miles an hour faster than it did before he worked on it. I asked him what he did, but Hugh doesn't talk much. 'I did a little of this and a little of that,' Hugh said."

Brad started the A-model, revved the engine up a little, looked at Bob and said, "Listen to that. Ever hear a motor run that smooth? Purrs like a kitten."

"Sure sounds smooth to me," Bob replied.

As they passed the Hipps Building on North Main, Bob pointed to the building and said, "There's where I'm staying."

Brad didn't say anything as he turned left and went around the back side of the paper mill. The river soon came into sight on the left side of the road. They crossed the bridge over Beaverdam Creek. This was all new country for Bob, and he was straining his eyes looking. He didn't want to miss anything just in case he had to come this way again.

"The road straight ahead goes up Smathers Hill," Brad said. "I hardly ever go that way. The hill is so steep, it's hard on the motor."

Brad kept to the road on his left, the one that followed the river. Several houses, sort of close together, were on the left side of the road. Brad motioned with his hand and said, "They call this settlement 'Peach Bloom'. I don't know why. I've passed through here many times, and I've never seen a peach tree with blooms. May have been some here before I was born. All the houses look like they are pretty old."

At the top of the hill Brad slowed down and said to Bob, "We turn right here. Straight ahead is goes into Buckeye Cove, and to your left is the Thickety Road."

Although Bob had watched everything along the road and was memorizing all the turns they made, he was beginning to doubt if he could ever find this place again. Neither one of them spoke for the next few minutes. Brad broke the silence when they were at the top of a small hill where three houses stood, two on the right and one on the left.

"This is where I live," Brad said. "They call this place 'Homebrew Knob'. Don't know why it has that name unless it's because everyone who has ever lived in these houses was associated with some kind of alcoholic drink."

Brad pulled his car along side of the house. "Get out and come in. I want you to meet Paul. This was his day to run the house. We take turns staying at home."

Brad turned the doorknob, but the door wouldn't open. Someone inside the house hollered, "Who is it?"

"That's Paul. He keeps the door locked when he's home. He must be afraid someone will sneak up on him," Brad told Bob.

"Open up! It's me, Brad. I brought someone with me I want you to meet," Brad said.

The door opened, and a lanky, black-headed young man said, "I didn't expect you back this early. I was sort of dozing a little while business is slow."

"Paul, I want you to meet my new friend, Bob. He's from Waynesville. Being from Waynesville yourself, you may have heard of him. He's the fellow that killed his wife a couple of years ago. He had to spend a year in jail. He's come to Canton looking for a job, but he has the same problem that you and I have: Nobody will give us a job because of our prison records."

Bob recognized the name "Pressley" right off. He remembered the Revenuers catching the Pressley boy who hauled moonshine and sending him to prison.

"Are you any kin to the Pressley boy who the Feds caught hauling lickker?" Bob asked Paul.

"Reckon so," Paul said to Bob. "That was my older brother, Ben Junior. He was named after Dad. He did a year up at a federal prison in Ohio in a town called 'Chilly' something or other. He let the Feds catch him on purpose. He wanted the Revenuers to move on, but they wouldn't leave until they caught someone, so he volunteered to be the one to get caught. He doesn't run moonshine anymore. Dad got too old to tend the still, so Ben took over making the lickker. He does a good job. He even doubles every batch just like Dad did. Everyone likes our corn lickker."

"I've got an idea," Brad said to Ben. "Why don't we get Bob to start working for us? He could tend to the sales here at home, and you and I both could be delivering to our bootlegger customers."

"I couldn't do that," Ben said. "We've only got one car."

"We'll buy another and get Hugh Wines to doctor it up a little to make it faster," Brad said.

"I sure appreciate the offer, but I'm afraid I'll have to turn it down," Bob said. "I want to find a steady job and start looking for a good woman and get married. I couldn't do this kind of work and raise a family. Thank you both for offering me the job, though."

Brad gave Bob a tour of the house and explained how they operated their "walk-in" business. He explained how they poured the whiskey from the half-gallon jars into half pint bottles called "bat wings". They sold them for fifty cents each. The pint size bottles sold for seventy-five cents each. He told Bob that most sales were of the bat wings for fifty cents each.

"Why don't we lock up the house and go to town for supper?" Brad said. "I've got to take Bob back, anyway. Wouldn't think of letting him walk back to town."

The three young men returned to town and headed straight to the Café. They didn't have to decide where they would eat supper because in Canton there was only one place besides the Hipps Boarding House, and that was the Café.

They went to a table off in the corner so they would have a little privacy. They talked about things that had happened in the past and what they had planned for the future. They enjoyed the meal as well as the friendship. They were somewhat like a family. But, Bob was still looking for some information about the Bluebird Gang.

"Do you think that the Bluebird Gang will ever get back together?" Bob asked Brad and Ben.

"I don't think that will ever happen. It was sort of foolish to do what we did. We took a big chance of getting into big trouble, and we didn't make any money. We couldn't sell the things we stole, and we gave most of it away, especially the candy. We were heroes to all the children we gave the candy to. They will miss the Bluebirds. They don't have money to buy candy."

Bob had the answer he was looking for. The Bluebird Gang was a thing of the past.

They finished their supper, finished talking, and said good-bye. Brad and Ben left in the Model-A Ford, and Bob went to his room in the Hipps Building. His job was finished. He had money left from the expense money. He decided not to walk back to Waynesville. He'd ride the Trailways Bus.

Bob was the first one at the table for breakfast the next morning. He wanted to get to the bus station early and find out when the next bus was going to Waynesville.

After Bob finished eating his breakfast he began to look for Mrs. Parks, the lady who ran the boarding house. He found her in the kitchen preparing vegetables to be cooked for the noon meal.

"Sorry to bother you," Bob said. "I just wanted to let you know that I will be leaving today."

"Whets the matter? Is there something you don't like about my boarding house?" she asked Bob.

"No, nothing's wrong. The room is nice, and you couldn't find any better food than you serve anywhere in the country."

"I don't give refunds on the rent," she told Bob.

"That's OK. I'm much obliged to you for letting me have the room. It sure beats staying at the hotel, and it's lots cheaper. If I ever come back to Canton and need a room, this will be the place I'll come to. Thanks again for keeping me."

Bob went to his room, packed the few things he'd

brought with him in the paper bag, left his room, and headed toward the bus station. He as he walked down the street, he thought about what he would tell the Sheriff when he got back to the Sheriff's Office in Waynesville.

The bus station was open for business when Bob arrived. He went in and walked up to the window where a sign read "Tickets and Information".

"When is the next bus that goes to Waynesville due?" Bob asked the man at the window.

He looked at the clock on the wall and said to Bob, "There is one due in thirty minutes. It's going all the way to Atlanta, Georgia."

"I'm not going to Georgia, only to Waynesville. How much is the ticket?" he asked.

The ticket-man ran his finger over a paper in front of him and said to Bob, "Seventy-five cents. How many do you want?"

Bob handed the ticket-man a dollar and said. "I only need one."

He handed Bob his ticket and a quarter change from the dollar bill Bob had given him. Bob took a seat at the bus station snack bar and ordered an orange drink.

"You'd better drink fast. They don't allow drinks on the bus, and it will be here in about fifteen minutes," the waiter said to Bob.

The bus was on time, and nearly all the seats had someone sitting in them. Bob found an empty seat about half-way back in the bus. There was a man in the seat by the window. He looked like he hadn't shaved for a couple of days, but he was dressed neatly in a sport coat and a white shirt without a neck tie.

It didn't take long for the bus driver to look the crowd

over, close the bus door, and pull back onto the road toward Waynesville.

"Where're you headed?" the man sitting by Bob asked.

"Waynesville -- about twelve miles up the road. Where are you going?" Bob asked him.

"I'm going to Atlanta. I've been on a bus for nearly two days. I left Baltimore day before yesterday. I'm sure getting tired."

This was Bob's first ride on a bus, and he looked it over, back to front. He also planned out what he would tell the Sheriff. He made up his mind that he was not going to tell how easy the investigation of the Bluebird Gang had been.

"Waynesville!" The bus driver called out.

Bob looked out the window to see where the bus station was. He had never had an occasion to visit it, and he didn't know where it was.

The bus stopped in front of a building with a sign above the door that read, "Bus Station". "This is Frog Level," Bob said. "Who would have ever thought a bus company would choose a building in Frog Level for their bus station in Waynesville?"

Bob was the only one to get off the bus. He had his bag of clothes under his arm, and he wasted no time heading toward the Sheriff's Office. He was anxious to see the Sheriff and tell him about the investigation in Canton.

Bob turned the doorknob to open the door to the Sheriff's Office. It didn't open. It was locked.

"I wonder where the Sheriff could be this time of the day?" Bob said to himself. "There must be at a meeting or something."

Bob took a key from his pocket and opened the door. "I'll unpack my clothes and wait a while before going to eat supper at the Café. I don't want to miss the Sheriff before he goes home for the day."

Bob had waited over two hours, and still there was no sign of the Sheriff. It was getting late in the day, and Bob was getting hungry.

"It'll soon be dark," thought Bob. "I'd better go eat and hurry back. The Sheriff may come by, and I'll miss him."

After supper bob returned to the jail, went to the room where his bed was, made it ready for the night, and went back to the office area. Still no Sheriff. He sat at the desk for over another hour and finally decided the Sheriff was not coming back to the office tonight.

"I guess I'll go to bed and get a good night's sleep. Maybe the Sheriff will come to work tomorrow morning. I haven't had a decent night's sleep since I left for Canton," Bob said..

The next morning, Bob was awakened by a noise in the office. He jumped out of bed, put his pants on, and headed to the office area. There stood the Sheriff.

"Sheriff, you're awful early this morning," Bob said.

"It's eight-thirty. I'm usually at work by eight. When did you get back?" the Sheriff asked.

"Around four yesterday. I looked everywhere for you. When I didn't find you, I was afraid something happened while I was gone. I'm glad to see you, Sheriff.

"Finish getting dressed, and we'll go eat breakfast. I want you to be good and awake when you tell me about your investigation of the Bluebird Gang," the Sheriff said to Bob.

Bob wanted to tell the Sheriff about what he did while they were eating, but the Sheriff stopped him.

"I want to hear the complete story from start to finish, so don't tell me anything until we get back to the office," the Sheriff said.

It was nearly ten o'clock when they returned to the office. The Sheriff sat down in his chair behind his big oak desk and said to Bob, "Get a chair and sit down up close to the desk and tell me what you did while you were in Canton. Don't leave anything out. I have to give the railroad people a report about the Bluebird Gang."

Bob began his report: "I guess you don't need to hear how I got to Canton or how I came back, so I will only give you the important part of what happened. I made contact with one of the members of the Bluebird Gang the first day I was in Canton.

"His name is Brad Hall. He recognized me from my name and was convinced that I was a criminal as bad, if not worse, than he is. I made friends with him, and during our conversation about our lives, he accidentally told me he was a member of what the railroad people call the Bluebird Gang. He told me there were three members: Jim Stone from Asheville, Paul Pressley from Waynesville, and him, Brad Hall from Canton. The Pressley boy is a brother to the Pressley who was sent to prison for hauling moonshine a while back. His name is Ben Junior, named after his dad. Paul said he let the Revenuers catch him so they would leave and quit bothering the other whiskey runners. That was the Bluebird Gang."

"What do you mean when you say, that 'was' the Bluebird Gang?" the Sheriff asked Bob.

"Well, they quit stealing. Brad said they couldn't sell

what the stole. They usually gave the candy to children and the cigarettes only sold for a nickel a pack. Jim Stone went back to Asheville. Brad Hall and Paul Pressley rented a house and are now bootleggers. Brad said they were doing real well. They have earned enough money to buy a souped-up Model-A Ford. They even offered me a job. Brad said they were foolish to ever steal from the trains and they stopped robbing them over two months ago.

"Well, Sheriff, you can tell the railroad people that you have broken up the Bluebird Gang, and that they will not have to worry about them anymore. The Bluebird Gang case is closed."

"You did a great job," the Sheriff said to Bob. "Next time I give the County Commissioners my budget, I'm asking for money to give you a raise. I couldn't have done a better job myself."

"Thank you," Bob said.

"You stay around the office while I'm gone. I'll go over to the train station and give them the good news. Maybe they will sleep better after they hear their trains are safe from thieves."

The Sheriff left the office with a big smile on his face. He was proud of the way his office had handled the case.

BANK
ROBBERS

The Sheriff and Bob were getting bored with nothing to do but sit around the jail and play checkers. The only law work they had done since the Bluebird case was handling complaints about missing chickens or family squabbles every now and then.

"I'm getting a little nervous. In fact, I'm kind of scared," the Sheriff said to Bob one day.

"What's bothering you? Bob asked.

"You've heard the old folks who live in these mountains predict the weather by the aches and pains in their bones," the Sheriff said. "It so happens that I can predict when there is going to be trouble in Haywood. Our lying around, playing checkers, and napping is going to cease, mark my word. I feel it in my bones. I feel like something is about to happen."

"I hope you're wrong," Bob said.

"I think I'll go visit the Pressley family. I haven't seen

Ben for quite some time. I'll tell him about your seeing his son in Canton and how well he's getting along. Ben is getting old and sort of worries about his boys. He quit running the still and lets the boys make the likker now. He still checks on them every now and then to see that they make the best moonshine in these mountains. I'll be back before quitting time," the Sheriff said.

Bob was glad to see the Sheriff leave. He was beginning to make him nervous by his fidgeting around and talking about trouble. Bob knew why the Sheriff decided to visit the Pressleys. He was getting low on his nerve tonic, the moonshine that he sipped on when got a little nervous. The Sheriff would offer Bob a sip about every time he had a drink, but Bob always refused. He had made a promise to his mom many years ago to never drink anything with alcohol in it.

Bob had a nap while the Sheriff was off visiting, but he was sweeping the office floor when he returned. Bob was right. The Sheriff had a big brown grocery bag under his arm. Bob knew what was in the bag, but he never let on that he even saw it. This same thing had happened many times since Bob moved to the jail.

"I told Ben you saw his boy over in Canton. He said for me to tell you 'howdy' and thank you for visiting Ben Junior. He sure is proud of his boys. He said he raised them right," the Sheriff said.

The Sheriff put the brown bag with its contents in the bottom drawer of his desk. He didn't bother to lock the drawer because he knew it would be safe with Bob around. He never mentioned it, but he was sure that Bob knew what he kept in this special drawer in his desk.

After a little drink of his nerve medicine, the Sheriff said to Bob, "See you tomorrow morning. I'm going home a little early. I've got a few things to do around the house. If you need me, give me a call at home."

Bob finished sweeping the office, put the papers on the Sheriff's desk in neat stacks, put the checkers and board away, and said to himself, "There. Everything looks a lot better."

After returning from the Café, Bob took a bath and was ready for bed. "These days of doing nothing sure make a feller tired. Guess I should have stayed a few more days in Canton. Could have done a lot of looking around. I may have met some girl who would make me a good wife. I hear tell there are lots of single girls in that end of the county. It's a little early but, I may as well go to bed," Bob said to himself as he turned down the blanket on his bed.

Bob was sort of tired of doing nothing. They didn't have much to do here. The Waynesville police got all the drunks and petty crimes in town. The Sheriff's Office covered all of Haywood County, including the towns, but the Sheriff usually let each town handle anything within their city limits. Of course, if something big happened, then the Sheriff and his Deputy would handle it.

The next morning Bob had been to the Café for breakfast and was straightening up his room when the Sheriff arrived. The time was nearly 8:30.

"I didn't get in any hurry this morning. It'll probably be another long day with nothing to do but play checkers and maybe doze a little," said the Sheriff. "But I've still got the feeling that something big is about to happen."

Suddenly the quiet was broken. The office door swung open, and Mr. Rogers, the local banker came through as though someone was after him. He was talking in a loud voice and thrashing his arms. Neither the Sheriff nor Bob could make out what was going on.

The Sheriff came from behind his desk, put his arm around Mr. Rogers' shoulders and said, "Calm down before you have a heart attack and tell me what's going on."

The banker calmed down enough to say, "Sheriff, I'm a ruined man. No one in this town will ever trust me or even speak to me. My bank was robbed last night. I don't know how much money they took, but it looks like all the money is gone. It wasn't my money. It belonged to the people who trusted me to keep it for them. Sheriff, I can't face my friends when they find out about their money being stolen."

The Sheriff pushed a chair toward Mr. Rogers and said, "Sit down, pull yourself together, and tell me exactly what you know about this bank robbery. Start at the beginning and don't leave anything out."

"I always get to the bank about thirty minutes before any of the employees get there," said Mr. Rogers. "This morning when I was opening the door I found it unlocked. I knew right then and there that something was wrong. In my forty years at the bank, I have never forgotten to lock the door. When I went inside, there were silver dollars scattered all over the lobby floor. I went straight to the safe vault and the door there was also open. I checked the shelves where the money boxes always sit, and several of them were gone. Then I knew for sure that my bank had been robbed. I locked the door to the bank and came straight here to you. The robber must have dropped the bag of silver dollars as he was leaving. The bag busted, and the dollars went all over the bank floor. The robber was in such a hurry to get out of the bank he didn't stop to pick them up. I don't know how much money they took."

"It looks like whoever robbed your bank knew a lot about it," said the Sheriff. "You go back to the bank and get things cleaned up before your employees get there. Don't tell them or anyone else about what happened. I'll contact the FBI and have them send someone to see me. If this robbery was done by someone here in Haywood, Bob and I will find them. If anyone acts different from their usual self or anyone asks questions, you let me know right away. Whoever robbed you may trap himself. And you quit your worrying about the money. It's all insured by the federal government. I have all the money I've saved for retirement in your bank, and I'm not worried. You leave everything to Bob and me, and we'll do our best to catch whoever took your money."

Mr. Rogers had calmed down a lot, but he still looked like someone who had seen a ghost. He was pale, and his eyes looked like they were run out on stems. He was in bad shape for a man his age. If the Sheriff hadn't calmed him down a little, he would have had a heart attack for certain.

As Mr. Rogers left the office the Sheriff turned to Bob and said, "Well, Bob, it looks like the vacation is over for a while. This is a lot bigger than the Bluebird Gang, and it will take a lot more planning and lots of long hours. Got any ideas for starters?"

"Well," Bob began. "There is one thing for sure, there're only a few ways to get out of these mountains. Either you go north toward Asheville, south toward Tennessee, or east toward Brevard. We can check these routes. There's not a lot of traffic on any of these roads, and if some strange car uses these roads it will be recognized as an outsider. We can ask the people living along these roads.

"Another thing is that Waynesville is a tourist town, and it will be hard to spot a suspect there. Yes sir, as you said, we've got a big job ahead. Our checker playing days are over for awhile. What plans do you have?" Bob asked.

"I think you'd better go over to Franks Cove and check at the apple house to see if they have seen any strangers headed toward Brevard. Then next go to the Balsam Lodge and check with the manager to see if anyone went toward Sylva. He would have seen him. I'll stay here in the office and call the Sheriffs in Asheville, Brevard, and Sylva and the police in Canton to let them know to be on the lookout for any strange cars leaving Haywood. There're no other ways out of these mountains unless someone goes by foot. I don't think anyone would try crossing any of the mountains around here. They're too rough and steep, and a person would never make it through the laurel thickets. We've got to be careful and not let anyone know the real reason we are looking for someone. You can take the A-model Ford because I won't need it here at the office."

The first plans for finding the bank robber were put into action. Bob was really happy about his assignment because he very seldom had the opportunity to drive the official Sheriff's car. Almost always only the Sheriff drove it. As he drove along the narrow, winding road to Franks Cove, he blew the oogah horn when someone waved at the Sheriff's car.

The cove was named after the Franks family. They owned all the land in the valley to the top of the mountain going toward the Bethel Community. And there were apple trees anywhere there was enough dirt to plant a tree. The mountain was very rocky as were the hills and valley below.

The apple house was located near the Franks family's homes. Most of the work taking care of the apples -- pruning, spraying, picking, and shipping -- was done by the men, women, and children of the Franks clan. Bob pulled the Ford up beside the apple house, set the parking brake, and got out. The elder Mr. Franks came out to greet him.

"Hello, Sheriff. What brings you to these parts?" he said to Bob.

"We're having some petty stealing going on over in town. I'm wondering if you happened to see any strangers over here or passing by in the last couple days," Bob said.

"Can't say that I have, but now that you mention it, I'm missing a couple of boxes of apples and three or four jugs of cider. You don't reckon the same feller stole them do you?" he asked Bob.

"I don't think so. It's too far to walk over here from town, and if a car came anywhere close to the apple house, you would see it. It must be some of the outside help you have. They wouldn't think it was stealing, just a part of their pay for their working here. You have the best cider in these parts," Bob said.

Bob shook hands with Mr. Franks and said, "Thanks for talking with me, and, if you do see a stranger, would you call the Sheriff's Office?"

"I sure will. Say, that's a good-looking Ford. Does it belong to you?"

"It belongs to the County. They bought it for the Sheriff. I use it every now and then. Well, I'd better get back to the office. I'll see you around," Bob said.

Bob decided to stop by the jail and check with the Sheriff before heading out to Balsam. He wanted to see if he had found out anything about the robber.

The Sheriff was on the telephone when Bob entered the jail. Bob tried to learn who the Sheriff was talking to and what he was saying, but the Sheriff was listening, not talking.

Bob sat down near the checker board while waiting for the Sheriff to finish his telephone call. He wanted to give him a report on the visit to the Franks' apple farm.

After a while, the Sheriff placed the telephone back on the hook. He turned toward Bob and asked, "What did you find out over in Franks Cove?"

"Mr. Franks said that no strangers had been around the apple house lately. He said that when the apples were ripe and for sale there were lots of strange people who came to buy apples and cider. They also bought sourwood honey, and when he had any, it was all gone in a day or two. He said he probably could sell any kind of honey as sourwood and the city folks wouldn't know the difference.

"I like to have never got away from Mr. Franks. He's getting old and wants to talk a lot. I guess he must be eighty or older. I enjoyed talking with him."

"I've just finished talking with the State Investigators over in Raleigh. I told them what happened and how we were keeping it quiet for a few days so we could investigate in our own way. They said that was OK, and if we needed them to help out just give them a call.

"I also called the FBI in Raleigh and told them what we are doing to locate the robber. They said that it was OK for us to try and solve the robbery, but they would have to come down to Waynesville and check out the bank. They said to keep word of the robbery from getting out. They're going to make arrangements with Mr. Rogers to look at the bank on a Saturday and Sunday when there's no one around."

The Sheriff and Bob were well on their way toward solving the bank robbery. Everything was going as they had planned.

"You'd better stop at the Café and get a bite to eat before you go to Balsam. There's nowhere to get anything to eat after you leave town. There're only a small grocery store and a post office on that mountain," the Sheriff said.

After Bob had finished his dinner at the Café, he headed out toward Balsam Mountain in the Model-A Ford. The only houses he saw along the road up the mountain were near the largest apple grower in Haywood County. Barker Orchards were well known throughout the eastern states. Barkers shipped apples as far north as New York City.

At the top of the mountain Bob turned onto a narrow dirt road crossed the Southern Railroad tracks, and passed the store and post office. He shifted into low gear on the Ford to go up the steep hill to the Balsam Hotel and Lodge.

The hotel was a large, two-story colonial-style building with a porch that circled the entire building. It was a very popular place for summer vacations for the wealthy from all over the South and some of the northern states. The southern-style meals that were served there three times daily and the cool summer weather on top of Balsam Mountain made it the perfect vacation spot in western North Carolina.

Bob hadn't come to Balsam for the good food and cool evenings. He had more important things to attend to. He parked the car, got out, and went inside to locate Mr. Fitzsimmons, the owner of the Balsam Lodge. He went to the small room that Mr. Fitzsimmons used for an office in back of the kitchen. The door to the office was open, and Bob knocked on the wall near the door.

Mr. Fitzsimmons looked up from whatever he was working on, saw the Sheriff's badge on Bob's shirt, and said, "Howdy Sheriff. What can I do for you?"

"I need some information if you have the time to spare for some questions," Bob said.

"I always have time to talk to our elected officials, especially the Sheriff. I hear a lot of good things about you and how you keep law and order in Haywood. Yes sir, it's always good to have a good Sheriff. It's the most important office in the County."

"I'm not the Sheriff. I'm the Deputy to the Sheriff," Bob said.

"That's OK. You are still a part of our county government. What kind of information do you want from me?" Mr. Fitzsimmons asked.

"We've had some reports around town of someone stealing. The Sheriff and I sort of suspect that it is someone who doesn't live here. We never have any trouble with our local people. Well, that is, uh, some of the younger boys will steal a chicken every once in a while so they and their sweethearts can have a 'chicken stew'. There's nothing wrong with that. That's been going on as far back as anyone can remember. It's just good clean fun so the young people will have something to do together."

"Me being raised up north, I never heard of a 'chicken stew'. It must be a lot of fun, and some good eating, too. I don't see anything wrong with that," Mr. Fitzsimmons said.

"The Sheriff sent me up here to ask you if you had noticed any strangers around here lately. That is, someone who is not a guest at your lodge," Bob said.

"I know most all of my out-of-town guests because they come back every summer. It's about the same bunch every year. I haven't seen anyone I don't know," he said.

"Well, I'd better get back to the Sheriff's Office. The Sheriff may have something else for me to do. Thanks for taking time to talk with me," Bob said as he headed toward the A-model.

"Come back any time," Mr. Fitzsimmons hollered to Bob.

As Bob was driving down Balsam Mountain toward Waynesville, he thought to himself, "I wish I could get more assignments like this. I get to see places I have never been to and meet some nice people I have never met. I might possibly meet a good woman who wants to get married."

While Bob was in his fancy world of dreams he took a wrong turn, and before he knew it he was on the road that went around Lake Junaluska. Lake Junaluska was part of a retreat where the Methodist Church held its annual meetings for all their churches throughout the USA.

The Sheriff

Bob found a wide place in the road, turned around, and headed the Ford toward Waynesville and the courthouse where the Sheriff's Office was located.

When Bob entered the office, he found the Sheriff at his desk talking on the telephone. He quietly found himself a chair and sat down. "I don't think the Sheriff saw me come in. Maybe if I listen close enough I'll be able to learn who he's talking to."

The Sheriff finally hung the telephone up, turned around in his swivel chair, and saw Bob sitting over near the door.

"I didn't know you were back," the Sheriff said. "I was talking with the FBI up in Raleigh. They're coming this weekend to do their investigation. They are going to keep it a secret for a couple of weeks so you and I will have a chance to find the robber. I don't want the news of the robbery to get out. Everyone might get scared about their money in the bank and want to take it out. If that happened, Mr. Rogers wouldn't have enough money to give them their savings."

"I wonder how much money the robber got," Bob said.

"Mr. Rogers said that the lady who does the accounting was told to keep the robbery a secret. She said that the bank was $50,003 short of what it should be. The robber took fifty packs of money. Each pack was one thousand dollars. The three dollars must be some of the silver dollars from among those that were scattered on the bank floor the morning after the robbery."

"You know something, Sheriff," Bob said. "Not taking all the money makes it look more like a local robber. He only took what he could hide somewhere and spend

103

without anyone noticing."

"Could be," said the Sheriff. "But who?"

"Like Mr. Fitzsimmons up at the Balsam Lodge said, they're not too many strangers around this time of the year. The tourist season is over," Bob said.

"Bob, go over to the bank and tell Mr. Rogers that I would like to talk with him. It'll be best if we talk here so no one can hear what we are talking about."

"I'll go to the bank and give Mr. Rogers your message, and on my way back I'll stop at the Café and eat dinner if it's OK with you. Do you want me to bring you anything from the Café?" Bob asked the Sheriff.

"No, I guess not. You hurry back in case Mr. Rogers comes over. I want you to hear everything he tells us. You may have some questions to ask him. Better get going," said the Sheriff.

When Bob arrived back at the office in the courthouse, Mr. Rogers was sitting in front of the desk talking with the Sheriff. When he saw Bob, he got up from his chair, put out his hand toward Bob and said, "Hello, Bob. I've been waiting 'til you got here before discussing the robbery".

The Sheriff began the conversation. "Have you noticed anything odd from your bank customers in the last few months? Do you have any new customers?"

"Well, I haven't noticed anything different with all of my old customers, but, come to think of it, the new feller who started banking with me about three months ago has asked me a lot of questions about the bank. I gave him a short tour of the bank, and he had a lot of questions. When I showed him the walk-in vault, he opened the door and made the remark that any money in the bank would be safe when the vault door was locked. I told him that the door hadn't been locked for over ten years and that the lock was broken. I told him that I close the vault door every night and everyone thinks it's locked."

"Did he ask about anything else?" the Sheriff asked.

"Well, let me think a minute. Oh, and he was talking about what a beautiful old building the bank was. He opened the front door to the bank, examined the big brass lock and door handle and muttered something that sounded like, 'Yale. Nineteen ten.' I asked him what he said, and he replied, 'Nothing. Just admiring the workmanship and material of this building.'"

"Who is this man and how did you meet him?" the Sheriff asked.

"About three months ago he came into the bank and asked to speak with the bank owner. The teller came into my office and said that I had a visitor. I told her to bring him into my office. He came into the office, we shook hands, and he introduced himself as Roscoe Alonzo from New York City. He said that he was on vacation and was staying at the Oak Tree Motel. He wanted to open a checking account for the summer. He counted out a thousand dollars, all in fifty-dollar bills. He said he would deposit more later. This is when he wanted to see the bank building."

"Have you seen him again this summer?" the Sheriff asked.

"Yes. Several times. But I never talked with him again until a week ago. I was out in the lobby when he came into the bank. He came over to where I was standing, put his hand out, and we shook hands.

"'I've decided to spend the winter here in Waynesville," he said. The motel gave me a great winter rate. I am going to New York for a couple of days next week, and when I return, I'll deposit some more money into my account. The people here in Waynesville are really friendly. They're never too busy to stop and talk awhile.'"

"Is that the last time you saw him?" the Sheriff asked.

"Yes. I don't know when he left for New York," said Mr. Rogers.

"Thanks for coming over and talking with us. Were trying to get your money back. If you hear anything unusual, let me know," the Sheriff said.

After the banker left the office, the Sheriff said to Bob, "Do you know any of the girls who work at the Oak Tree Motel? I have heard you mention several times that they eat at the Café where you do."

"Yes, several of them eat there, especially Fanny. She eats all of her meals at the Café. We have shared the same table several times. Come to think of it, she has mentioned that feller, Alonzo. She said that she usually took care of his room and that he was a big tipper. He usually gave her five dollars just to clean his room. She said he was sort of odd. He only wanted her to do the cleaning. He changed the sheets and made his own bed."

"When you go to eat supper, be sure to sit with her. Find out all you can about our Mr. Alonzo. We may be on our way to solving this bank robbery," the Sheriff said.

When Bob went to the Café for his supper, he saw Fanny sitting alone at a table off in the corner of the Café. He went to her table and said, "Mind if I eat with you? It's kind of lonely eating alone."

"I'd be happy for you to join me. I don't like to eat

alone either," Fanny said to Bob.

While Fanny and Bob were waiting for the waiter to bring their supper, they talked about the weather, what they did that day, and other little things. Bob waited for the right time to question her about Mr. Alonzo. There was no reason to pressure her. Everything had to be casual if he got any information from her. The workers at the motel were told that they should never give anyone any information about the guests staying at the motel. Bob didn't want to cause Fanny any trouble that could lead to her losing her job.

Fanny and Bob had finished their meal and were sipping on their iced tea. "Are you still cleaning the room for that feller from New York?" Bob asked Fanny.

"I clean it when he is in the room. He told the manager to not let anyone in his room when he was not there. He left a couple of days ago. He didn't mention where he was going. Sort of strange, he gave me a ten dollar tip and told me to be sure that no one went in his room while he was gone. Not even me."

Bob said to Fanny, "Well, see you tomorrow," and then he left the Café and returned to the courthouse.

"Well, what did you find out?" the Sheriff asked Bob.

Bob told the Sheriff about Alonzo being sort of strange-acting about his bed and his not wanting anyone bothering it.

"The FBI will be here this weekend to look the bank over to see if they can come up with a clue about the robbery," the Sheriff said to Bob. "I want them to get fingerprints off the vault door and also the trays that the money is stored in. From what Mr. Rogers told us, Alonzo's prints will be on the vault door, but they shouldn't be anywhere else in the vault. We may be on the right track in solving the robbery, but we've got to be careful. Remember that," the Sheriff said. "We could get in big trouble if we arrest the wrong person."

The FBI came by the Sheriff's Office on Saturday morning to check with him about what he had found out about the robbery. The Sheriff didn't tell the FBI what he knew about the man from New York, Mr. Alonzo. He did remind them that he would like copies of the fingerprints they found on the doors and in the vault.

After the FBI men left the Sheriff's Office, the Sheriff said to Bob, "I guess we'd better figure out how we can search that room where Mr. Alonzo is staying at the Oak Tree Motel. We need to find the reason for him not wanting anyone in his room when he is not there. And why he changes the sheets on his bed instead of letting Fanny change them. And why he takes these trips to New York every few weeks."

"Well, Sheriff," Bob said, "Fanny told me that the manager gave orders that no one was to go near Mr. Alonzo's room while he is away. As I see it, we would have to get a search warrant, and that would let the cat out of the sack. It wouldn't be a secret anymore, and the whole county would be running to the bank to check on their money. We have to find some other way to get in that room, and get in there before Mr. Alonzo returns from his trip."

"Guess you are right," the Sheriff said to Bob. "We are forced to tell the manager at the motel what we need to do. Maybe he'll keep it a secret about the bank being robbed. It's not very far to the motel from here, so I'll walk up there instead of taking the car. No one will notice me but they would be wondering why the Sheriff's car was at the motel if I drove over."

"Good thinking," the Sheriff said. Go ask the manager if he would come to my office. Tell him it's real important and to come as soon as he can. And you come straight back. I need you here when I tell him what we want to do. And if you see Fanny, don't hang around talking to her. She may get suspicious."

Bob and Mr. Owens, the motel manager, arrived at the Sheriff's Office about the same time. The Sheriff didn't expect to see Mr. Owens come to his office this quickly, but he was glad he did.

"I hate to be a bother to you, Mr. Owens, but I have something that has to be done right away, and I need your help."

"I'll be glad to be of help any way I can," said Mr. Owens. "What do you want from me?"

"First, I need your word that you will not discuss what we talk about with anyone. This is very important. I hope you will understand," the Sheriff said.

"You have my word on it, Sheriff," Mr. Owens said.

The Sheriff told Mr. Owens about the bank robbery and that he needed to search Mr. Alonzo's room while he was away. He explained that he had reason to suspect him as being the robber or a part of the robbery. He didn't go into details as to why he suspected him. "I need to do the search as soon as possible," he said.

"Would about six o'clock tonight be early enough?" Mr. Owens asked the Sheriff. "All the employees will be gone except the night clerk, and she will be busy in the office. His room is on the back side of the motel, and I will meet you there so no one will see us together if that is OK with you."

"That would suit me just fine. Bob and I will be there at six on the dot. Sure appreciate your helping us and keeping it quiet," the Sheriff said.

When the Sheriff and Bob arrived at the motel, the manager, Mr. Owens, was standing at the door to the room that the New York fellow, Mr. Alonzo, had rented for the rest of the year.

"The door is unlocked," Mr. Owens said to the lawmen.

"You'd best wait outside," the Sheriff said to the manager. I don't want you to see anything in case we do find something. If you did you would have to be a witness if Alonzo is tried."

"Suits me fine. I don't want to get involved in court trials," he said.

The Sheriff and Bob opened the door, entered the room, stood still for a minute, and gave the room a good look. The Sheriff started looking around on one side of the room and Bob the other. They opened a few drawers in the dresser and other furniture in the room. They next approached the bed, one of them on either side. They slowly removed the blanket and sheets from the bed. Next they removed the mattress.

"Wow! Look at that," Bob hollered. "I see why Alonzo wouldn't let Fanny make the bed when she cleaned this room. I never saw this much money in my whole life."

The Sheriff was speechless. It was more than a minute before he spoke. I guess we've found the bank robber. The bands around the bundles of money have the bank's name on them. I wonder how much money there is on that bed spring?" the Sheriff said to Bob.

"Be afraid to say," Bob replied.

"Tell Mr. Owens to come in. It would be best to have a witness after all. You stay here and guard the money in case our robber comes back from his trip a little early. I'll call the FBI and tell them what we have here and ask them what we should do with the money. Robbery of a bank is a federal offence, so this makes them in charge from here on out."

The Sheriff returned to his office in the courthouse, telephoned the FBI office in Raleigh, and told them what he and Bob had found in the motel room, and he asked them what he should do with the money.

"Put all the money in a box or sack and take it to the bank. Don't let anyone touch it. Have someone stay in the motel room until we get there. Best to have two people in the room just in case your robber comes back. Give us a description of what he looks like, and we will start an all out search for him. Don't let anyone go near the room, and keep things as quiet as you can. If this Alonzo fellow gets wind of your finding the money in his room, he will hide out. Be careful. He may be dangerous. I'll be there as soon as I can. It'll probably be around midnight when I arrive."

"I don't know what the suspect looks like, but if you will call Mr. Rogers, the bank president, he knows exactly what he looks like. He gave the agent Mr. Rogers' home telephone number. I'll be waiting for you," said the Sheriff.

The Sheriff returned to the motel where Bob and the manager were waiting. He told them the instructions that the FBI had given him and that he had a problem: Where was he going to get that second man to stay with Bob and guard the room?

The Sheriff gave Mr. Owens a good look. "Mr. Owens, I need another favor from you. Would you stay with Bob until the FBI gets here? I'll deputize you and give you my pistol for protection."

"I've never done a lot of shooting, but guess I could if I had to. And I feel sort of bad that I rented one of my rooms to this bank robber. I'll do it," he said.

Mr. Owens was sworn in as a Deputy of the Sheriff's Office, given the pistol that the Sheriff always carried and given orders to turn out all the lights and stay inside.

The Sheriff returned to the office, called Mr. Rogers the banker, and asked him to come to the Sheriff's Office as soon as he could. He told the banker it was very important.

When Mr. Rogers arrived the Sheriff told him what he found at the motel and that he needed boxes to carry the money in and that no one was to touch the money after it was back in the bank.

The Sheriff and Mr. Rogers went to the bank in the Sheriff's Model-A Ford. Mr. Rogers opened the door and went into the bank and within five minutes returned with two metal boxes. They went to the motel, and the Sheriff knocked on the door of Alonzo's room.

"Bob, this is the Sheriff and Mr. Rogers. Open the door. We brought boxes to take the money to the bank in."

Bob opened the door. They placed the boxes the bed, and the four of them packed all the money into the two boxes. They looked all around the room to be sure that none of the money had been overlooked. They put the boxes of money in the Ford and were soon on their way to the bank to leave the money for safe-keeping. Bob and the new Deputy closed the door and turned the lights off. Everything was falling into place in solving the bank robbery, but the big job was still ahead: catching Mr. Alonzo, the robber.

After the money was back in the bank, the Sheriff and Mr. Rogers went to the Sheriff's Office in the courthouse to wait for the FBI.

"We may as well play a game of checkers while we wait," the Sheriff said. "It'll be another three or four hours before the federal men get here. What color do you want?"

The checker game was under way when the banker asked the Sheriff, "How do you think Alonzo opened the door to the bank, Sheriff?"

"Do you recall telling me about the first time he came to the bank and how you gave him the tour? Remember him giving the lock on the front door a good going over and hearing him mumble the name 'Yale' and some numbers? As I figure it, he took the number from the lock, sent it to the Yale lock company with a letter about losing the key. They mailed him a key, and the rest was easy."

"Yeah, and he had a big smile on his face when I told him the lock was broken on the vault door. I never dreamed that I was helping him with his plans to rob the bank. I'll never let anyone behind the counter in the bank as long as I live," Rogers said to the Sheriff.

After ten or twelve checker games and four hours of waiting, two FBI agents arrived at the Sheriff Office. The Sheriff didn't waste any time. He took them to the motel. Bob opened the door when the Sheriff told him who they were. Everyone went inside the room. The agents looked around and especially at the bed where the stolen money was found.

"You and your deputies can go home and get some sleep. My partner and I will stay here the rest of the night. Two of you come and relieve us about eight tomorrow morning," one of the agents said to the Sheriff."

The Sheriff told Mr. Owens to be at his office by seven o'clock the next morning. "Go home and get a little sleep if you can," he said to his Deputy.

"Go to bed," the Sheriff said to Bob. "I think I'll have a little nap on the cot in one of the cells. If I go home I'll have to come straight back. The night's nearly gone. It'll be daylight before you know it."

The next morning after Bob and the motel manager relieved the two federal agents, they came to the Sheriff's Office.

"Where can we get a bite to eat?" one of the agents asked the Sheriff.

"Go across the street, turn right toward the fire hall. The Café is two blocks up the street. They are open; the Café never closes. They have pretty good food, especially their breakfast," the Sheriff said.

The two federal men came back to the Sheriff's Office in about thirty minutes.

"I need to use your telephone," the agent who did most of the talking said to the Sheriff.

"Help yourself. Here, take my chair. I guess you are tired after being up all night."

The agent picked up the telephone, dialed the operator, and said, "Would you connect me with 555-2626 in Raleigh?"

The telephone on the other end rang, and everyone

was as quiet as a mouse. They wanted to hear what was being said.

"FBI office. Tom Henson speaking. Can I help you?"

"Good morning, Chief. Sam Bailey here. Anything on the Alonzo fellow we suspect robbed the bank here in Waynesville?"

"Yes. We think we spotted him getting on the bus going to Asheville. We didn't want him to know that we were getting watching him. We decided to lay back and see where he was going after he arrived in Asheville. Sometimes this is best. They will return to their home. He'll be watched every minute. It looks like he has a friend traveling with him. Better have someone stationed at the motel in case he returns. Better be careful, he may be armed and dangerous. Good luck."

Agent Sam Bailey hung the telephone up. The office was so quiet you could have heard a pin drop. "Did you hear what the Chief said?"

They nodded their heads and answered, "yes."

"Here is the plan," Agent Bailey said. "Your Deputy and I will hide inside the motel room. My partner and the other Deputy will hide outside where they can see anyone who enters the room. The Sheriff will stay here at the office should a call come in from one of our agents. If the suspect is returning to Waynesville, it will be around noon when he gets here. Let's hope we get our bank robber."

Everyone took his position at the motel. Bailey made the bed to look like it had never been touched. They locked the door and looked around for a good hiding place.

"When we hear someone at the door we'll hide in the bathroom," Bailey said to Bob. "We've got to move fast once he is inside. We don't want him to escape and sure don't want him to shoot you or me."

It was nearing twelve-thirty when Bob and the agent heard someone at the door. They hurried into the bathroom and closed the door. "This is it," Bailey whispered to Bob.

"Everything looks just like it did when I left," Bob and Bailey heard someone say. "Give me a hand moving this mattress from the bed. We'll get the money and head back to New York."

The FBI Agent tapped Bob on the shoulder and placed his finger over his mouth to indicate silence. Next, he took his pistol from its holster and motioned for Bob to do the same. He then held three fingers up and slowly closed one at a time. When the third finger was closed Bailey opened the bathroom door, and he and Bob rushed out with their guns in their hands.

"Freeze! FBI!" Bailey yelled. "You move and you are dead."

The door to the room opened, and in came the other FBI agent and Mr. Owens, the motel manager and newly appointed Deputy.

"Mr. Alonzo! Mr. Shenk!" Owens hollered.

"Do you know these men?" Agent Bailey asked Mr. Owens.

"Mr. Shenk was a guest for two weeks this past summer, and Mr. Alonzo was here all summer and was staying on for the winter."

"Put the cuffs on them," Bailey said to his partner. "We'll keep them in the Haywood County Jail until they send a prisoner transportation car from Raleigh. Drive our car around back. I don't want everyone in town seeing them walking into the courthouse."

When the Sheriff saw the agents and his deputies bringing two handcuffed men into his office, he jumped up and said, "You caught him. You have two men. What happened?" He was as excited as a kid on Christmas morning.

"It seems that Mr. Alonzo had a partner when the bank was robbed," Bailey said. "We will know when he is fingerprinted. We got some good prints from the bank vault."

The next day a truck with a cage for transporting prisoners arrived at the courthouse in Waynesville. The two suspected bank robbers were locked in the cage and soon on their way to the federal prison.

Bailey, the FBI agent, asked the Sheriff to have everyone who knew about the robbery to come to the courthouse. He wanted to meet with them to let them know what they could expect later when a trial was held for the prisoners.

Bob was assigned this job by the Sheriff. He didn't mind telling Mr. Rogers and the others, but he sure dreaded telling Fanny, the girl who worked at the motel. He liked Fanny and didn't want to lose her friendship. But he had to tell her, hoping she would understand and not get mad at him.

The meeting time was at ten o'clock the next morning. Everyone was on time, and FBI agent Bailey asked them to have a seat. Extra chairs were brought in to the Sheriff's Office for the meeting. Everyone who had knowledge of the bank robbery was there. Fanny was the only woman at the meeting, and she chose to sit beside Bob.

Agent Bailey went to the front of the room, introduced himself, and thanked them for coming to the meeting.

"The trial of the suspected robbers will not be held here in Waynesville where the crime was committed," Bailey said. "Bank robbery is a federal offence, so they will be tried in federal court. I don't know where trial will be. It could be in Charlotte, Raleigh, or even Asheville. When they have a hearing, a judge will set the time and place for the trial.

"If they should plead guilty, there will not be a trial, but a date for sentencing them will be set. But if they plead not guilty there will be a trial with a jury. This means that some of you will have to attend the trial as witnesses. It may be that all of you will be called by the federal lawyers to tell what you know about the robbery.

"Do not discuss this matter or give anyone any information about the robbery. Don't even talk among yourselves about it.

"Sheriff, Mr. Rogers, I want you to count the money that you found in the motel and send me a report giving the amount. Do this as soon as you can. I'm going to push for a speedy trial, I and need to have everything ready.

"Before we leave, I want to say that you have one of the best Sheriffs, if not the best, in North Carolina. He and his Deputies did a great job in solving this robbery in such a short time. Thank you, Sheriff Harbin. Meeting adjourned."

Bob walked to the door with Fanny and said, "Thank you for helping me. I'll see you at the Café."

FUTURE SHERIFF

Everything was back to normal at the Sheriff's Office. The money found at the motel had been counted by the Sheriff and Mr. Rogers, the banker. All of the money that was missing from the bank after the robbery was accounted for plus an extra three hundred and twenty four dollars. The Sheriff asked Mr. Rogers to keep the extra money until he filed his report with the FBI agent.

"When I get this report finished and in the mail to the FBI, we'll play a game of checkers," the Sheriff said to Bob.

"Fine with me. I may let you win," Bob teased.

Sheriff Harbin looked toward Bob, smiled, and then back to work on the report.

He finished the report to the FBI, sealed it in an envelope and handed it to Bob. "Take this to the post office and get it in the mail. Hurry back, and we'll get that checker game started."

Bob wasn't gone more than thirty minutes when he returned to the office. The Sheriff already had the checker board set up with the checkers in place.

"What color do you want?" he asked Bob.

"Don't make any difference. I'll beat you with either color," Bob said to the Sheriff.

"Better not brag. You may have to eat crow," the Sheriff said to Bob.

After the two lawmen had played five or six games of checkers, the Sheriff said to Bob, "It's nearly dinner time, so we better quit. You go to the Café and eat, and when you get back I have a little visit planned. I'll stop at my house and have a bite to eat then go on for my visit. If you run into Fanny don't spend a lot of time talking to her. When I leave I probably won't be back to the office until tomorrow morning. You will have to take care of the Sheriff's Office for the rest of the day."

"Not trying to be nosey, but I need to know where you will be just in case something comes up that I can't handle by myself," Bob said."

"I'm going to pay Ben Pressley a little visit. I haven't seen him in quite some time. Ben carries a lot of weight when election time comes. About everyone on the ridges and in the hollers of the mountains around Haywood votes the way Ben votes. Mighty fine man, that Ben."

Bob wasn't fooled at all. He knew the main reason that the Sheriff was paying Ben Pressley a visit: He was getting low on what he called his 'nerve medicine', or he was completely out. Ben Pressley was known for making the best moonshine in North Carolina, and Tennessee, to boot. He ran a clean still, and he also doubled his moonshine. His son Ben Junior did most of the work now that

Ben Senior was getting old.

The Sheriff did need to restock his supply of nerve medicine, but he also had other business to discuss with Ben. He would tell Bob what it was all about when the right time came. He had plans that no one else knew about.

Ben Pressley was sitting in his favorite cane-bottom chair on his porch when the Sheriff arrived. Not many of the log houses in these mountains had a porch. Ben's house was one of the few.

"Howdy Sheriff," Ben said to Sheriff Harbin as he walked toward the house. "Pull up a chair and visit a spell. Haven't seen you in a while. Where you been keeping yourself?" Ben Pressley was asking more questions than the Sheriff could answer.

"Good to see you, Ben," the Sheriff said. "You're looking well. How have things been going? How is the family?" The Sheriff was all wound up with questions for Ben, also.

Ben and the Sheriff shook hands. The Sheriff found himself a chair and sat down near Ben.

"I've been aiming to visit sooner, but I didn't have time. We had a bank robbery downtown, and we had to catch the robber. Bob and I worked around the clock, and it paid off. Not only did we catch the feller that robbed the bank; we got all the money back, plus a little extra.

"Speaking of Bob, my Deputy, what do you think of him as a law man?"

"I don't really know much about him," Ben said. "I only know what you have told me and what my boy who lives in Canton said about him. I can't fault him for killing his wife. Maybe she had it coming to her. My boy

Paul took a liking to him when he met him in Canton. Why do you ask me about him? Is he in trouble or something?"

"Before I talk to you about what I have on my mind, I want your word that you won't mention what I tell you to anyone. I haven't told anyone about my plans. I haven't mentioned it to my family or Bob."

"You have my word," Ben said.

"I don't know where to start telling you my plans, so first off I'll tell you why I've been thinking for a long while about retiring from this Sheriff's job. My problem is that I don't know who to turn the Sheriff's Office over to. I don't have any boys. Just the two girls. The only one I can think of that would make a good Sheriff is my Deputy, Bob."

"Didn't he serve some time in jail?" Ben asked.

"Yes, but Bob didn't kill his wife, Sally."

"Ben, I'll tell you what happened and why Bob pleaded guilty at his trial. Sally made it look like Bob killed her but he didn't touch her."

The Sheriff told Ben all about finding Bob's blue tick hound in the grave and about going to Haysville finding Sally and her telling how she killed Old Blue and making Bob think he'd killed her.

"But no one else in Haywood knows this. They all believe Bob killed his wife," Ben said.

"I know," the Sheriff said. "I'll figure out some way to let everyone know the truth. I should have straightened this mess out a long time ago. It was my responsibility to have investigated this before the trial, but I didn't. Bob served a year in jail that he didn't deserve. And it was all my fault because I didn't do my duty as Sheriff of Haywood County."

"Don't put yourself down, Sheriff," Ben said. "We all make mistakes every now and then. You'll figure out something, I'm sure."

"When election time comes around there will be several on the ballot for Sheriff. In the last few years several families who came to the mountains for the summer months didn't go back home. They have made their home here and have big ideas about how our county should be run. We don't need some outsider telling us what to do and trying to change the way we live. This is why I want to get someone on the ballot who can win the Sheriff's job after I retire."

"Have you talked to Bob about him becoming the Sheriff?" Ben asked.

"No. Like I said, you are the only person I have talked to about this. I'll talk with Bob soon. I hope he agrees to run for Sheriff and get on the ballot next spring.

"I hate to leave so soon, but it's getting up in the day. Better get off this mountain before dark. I enjoyed the visit. Oh, I about forgot, I'm running a little low on my nerve tonic. I better get a couple of jars if you have any to spare. Sure helps settle my nerves when things get a little out of hand."

Ben got up from his chair and walked toward the door and into the house. He was gone only a few minutes and returned to the porch with a tow-sack in his hand. He handed it to the Sheriff and said, "Are you sure two jars will be enough? I just finished this batch last night. Sure turned out real good. Made the mash with yellow sweet corn. Course you don't see the yellow. It turns out as clear as spring water. But it sure has a good flavor. Guess

I'll get a quarter more on the jar."

"How much do I owe you?" the Sheriff asked.

"You don't owe me anything. I have never charged the Sheriff of Haywood County for his whiskey. My pa never did charge them either. When they come here they know what they are getting. The best moonshine in the country comes from the Pressley still. I hope it settles your nerves," Ben said.

Sheriff Harbin thanked Ben for the likker, laid it in the backseat of the A-model and headed home. All the while he was thinking of a way to get the news out about Bob not being a murderer. Bob knew about it, but no one else knew that Bob didn't kill Sally.

When the Sheriff went to his office the next morning he didn't mention to Bob anything about his plans. Everything was normal, including a couple of checker games. Even while the checker games were being played, the Sheriff was in deep thought about a plan to tell the voters of Haywood County about the mistakes he made when Bob told him he had killed his wife Sally. He should have had an autopsy and a death certificate to verify that she was dead. But he didn't, and Bob pleaded guilty and had to spend a year in jail. "I didn't do my job the way I should've," he said to himself.

"Wonder when the trial will be for the bank robbers," Bob said to the Sheriff.

The Sheriff sat up straight in his chair, looked at Bob, smiled and said, "That's the answer. You just gave me the answer."

"Answer to what?" "Bob asked.

"Oh, nothing. I was just thinking out loud," he said to Bob.

When they finished the checker game, the Sheriff stood up and stretched his arms and said to Bob, "Too near dinner time to play another game. How about your eating a little early today? I need to go talk with someone this afternoon, and you need to look after things while I'm gone."

"No problem with that," Bob said. "I'll wash up a bit and go eat."

"If you see Fanny, don't get carried away with her. I need you back as soon as you finish your dinner."

Bob did happen to see Fannie at the Café. He waved at her and said hello, but he didn't start a conversation. He hurriedly ate his lunch and headed back toward the office in the courthouse.

"The Sheriff must have something very important to take care of." He was all excited about me hurrying back so he could go do whatever he had planned."

When Bob opened the door to the office the Sheriff already had his hat and coat on and was ready to leave.

"I may not get back today," he said to Bob. "If I don't come back, I'll see you tomorrow morning." He was gone before Bob could say anything.

Bob didn't know it, but the Sheriff was still in the courthouse. He was at the Judge's Office. It was the Judge who was on the bench when Bob was tried for murdering his wife Sally.

"Would you tell the Judge that Sheriff Harbin would like to see him?" he said to the Judge's secretary.

She picked up the telephone, pushed a button, and waited for an answer.

"Yes," the Sheriff heard someone say. "Sheriff Harbin is here and would like to see you."

"Send him in," he heard the Judge say.

"You can go in. The Judge will see you," the secretary said.

The Sheriff went into the Judge's office. They shook hands and greeted each other.

"Good to see you, Sheriff. I haven't seen you since the murder trial a couple of years ago. What brings you here?"

"Well, Judge, I've got a problem, and I think you are the only one who can really help me with it."

"What's your problem, then?" the Judge asked.

"It's about the trial of Bob Boyd. I don't know where I should start, but the bottom line is that I want to let the people of Haywood County know the truth about Bob. He didn't kill his wife. It was all a mistake, and the mistake was caused by my not doing my job as I should have. I didn't look into the matter. I took Bob's word when he said he had killed his wife."

"Whoa, slow down", the Judge said. "Start at the beginning and go a little slower with your story."

The Sheriff found a chair, sat down, and took a deep breath.

"Sorry, Judge. I guess I'm a little bit excited about telling you what really happened."

"That's OK. Take your time. I don't have anything important on my schedule for the rest of the day. Tell me what you found out about this case."

The Sheriff started at the beginning telling the Judge about where he found Bob burying what he thought was his wife and about what they found when Bob was giving Sally a decent funeral at the Baptist Church graveyard. He went on to tell about the investigation over at

Haysville where he found Sally and about what she told him about the day of the 'murder' at their home on the mountain.

"Why haven't you come to me sooner with this new evidence?" the Judge asked. He seemed a little upset with the Sheriff.

"Well, when Bob and I found out the truth and learned how I had made the mistake by not investigating, Bob wanted to keep it quiet. He said it wouldn't bring back the year he spent in jail and it would make me look bad."

"Why are you bringing this up now?" the Judge asked.

The Sheriff explained to the judge about his plans to retire and about getting Bob on the ballot for Sheriff.

"How can I get word out to the people about Bob not being a murderer?" he asked the Judge.

The Judge looked at the ceiling, scratched his head, and looked straight at the Sheriff and said, "You've kind of got a messy problem here, but I think we can get it cleared up. It won't be easy, it but can be done."

"What can I do?" the Sheriff asked.

"As I said, it'll not be easy, but it can be done. It will take something sort of like a new trial without lawyers and witnesses or spectators in the court room," the Judge said.

"What can I do to help?" the Sheriff asked.

"The first thing is to find a couple of days when I could work a hearing into my schedule. Next is to get that woman, Sally, up here from Haysville to tell me what happened between her and Bob, her ex-husband. That will be your job: getting her here once I set the date," the

Judge said.

"It may take some doing to get Sally to come to Waynesville. She wouldn't talk to me when I found her until her dad made her tell me what happened. I may have to get a warrant to get her here."

"I'll let you know in a day or two when we can have the hearing. I would like to keep this between you and me until the day we have the hearing," the Judge said.

"Let me hear from you as soon as you set the date, and I'll drive over to Haysville and have a talk with Sally and her dad. They'll probably need a couple of days' notice. I may have to take a court order in case Sally refuses to come to Waynesville for the hearing," the Sheriff said to the Judge.

The next morning when the Sheriff arrived at his office, Bob was still cleaning up and getting everything in its place.

"When you get through with your work, we'll finish the checker game that we were playing yesterday when I had to leave," the Sheriff said.

Bob noticed how calm the Sheriff was this morning. He either had a big dose of his nerve medicine before coming to work, or he had the problem solved that was bothering him. "This is going to be a good day," Bob thought to himself. When the Sheriff was in this kind of mood, there would always be several checker games, and the Sheriff would win most of them. He loved to play checkers.

The following day the Judge called the Sheriff and gave him the date for the hearing about getting Bob's murder record straightened out. He would hear testimony from Sally on Tuesday and Wednesday of the next week.

"Have Sally and Bob at my office by nine o'clock Tuesday morning. I'll take care of all the other details," he had told the Sheriff.

The Sheriff was anxious for everyone to know that sending Bob to jail for killing his wife was a mistake. He would have Sally in the Judge's office regardless of what he had to do to bring her from Haysville.

"Bob, I guess it's about time to tell you what I am doing and why the Judge called me. I have been thinking about retiring sometime soon, and it bothers me about your serving a year in jail for something you didn't do. I feel bad about this because I didn't do my duty as Sheriff. I don't want you to have to carry the name of a murderer for the rest of your life. I want everyone in this county and anywhere else to know that you did not kill your wife, Sally.

"The Judge has agreed to have a hearing and get this all straightened out. I have to bring Sally here from Haysville so she can give the judge her story of what took place up at your house on the mountain the day you thought you'd killed her. You will have to be there for the hearing, too."

"Aw, Sheriff, you don't have to go to all this trouble just to let people know that I didn't kill Sally. She's back home with her dad and sisters, I have a good job, and everyone knows that I wouldn't harm anyone," Bob said.

"I'll not come to the office tomorrow. I'm driving over to Haysville to tell Sally to be here next Tuesday morning for the hearing. I'll come by the office if I get back before five o'clock. I don't think you will have any problem taking care of things around here," the Sheriff said to Bob.

It was a beautiful day for the drive over to Haysville,

and the Sheriff planned how he would give the news to Sally about her coming trip to Waynesville. He knew it would not be easy to get her to promise that she would be there for the hearing.

"Well, this is it," the Sheriff said to himself as he turned off the highway into the driveway leading to the Ensleys' house. "And there's Big John and two of his daughters sitting on the porch." Everything looked the same as it did the day he left to go back to Waynesville from his fishing trip a while back.

When the Sheriff got out of his car, the two girls left the porch and went into the house. Big John Ensley put his hand above his eyes and leaned forward to see who his visitor was. When he recognized who it was, he sat back in his chair and waited until the Sheriff was closer to the porch.

"Hello there, Sheriff," Big John said. What brings you back down here? Did you bring your fishing pole? Pull up a chair and make yourself at home."

"I didn't come to fish this time. I have a little business to talk to you about," the Sheriff said.

"What's on your mind?" Big John asked.

The Sheriff told Big John about the hearing and that Sally had to go to Waynesville for a couple of days to tell the Judge about what happened the day she left Bob and came back home.

"If I can talk to Sally, maybe she will agree to come to the hearing."

Big John got up from his chair and said to the Sheriff, "Let's go in the house, and you can talk to her. She's a little stubborn sometimes. I guess she got it from her mama. Have a seat on the sofa," John said to the Sheriff after they were inside.

"Sally, come in here. The Sheriff wants to talk with you."

"I don't want to talk to the Sheriff," Sally hollered back to her dad.

"You get in here this minute. You hear me?"

Sally entered the living room and sat in a chair on the opposite side of the room from the Sheriff.

"Sally," the Sheriff began. "Bob is going to run for Sheriff and the Judge has agreed to hear your story of what took place the day that Bob thought he killed you. This will clear him of being a murderer. All you have to do is be at the Judge's Office next Tuesday morning, tell him your story, and come back home."

"I'm not going," Sally said. "I don't want to see any Judge, and I shore don't want to see that Bob Boyd ever again."

"I'm afraid you don't have a choice," the Sheriff said. "If you don't volunteer to go, the Sheriff here in Haysville will arrest you and bring you to my jail in Waynesville. I have a court order from the Judge to see that you are in his office next Tuesday morning. I was hoping I wouldn't have to use it, but I will if necessary. You can bring your dad along if you want to. You can come by bus, or if you would like for me to come get you on Monday, I will. You can spend the night at the Oak Tree Motel and eat your meals at the Café. I will pay all of your expenses for this hearing."

"Sheriff," Mr. Ensley said, "you can come over on Monday, and we will be ready to go to Waynesville. Don't worry about Sally not being there for the hearing. I give you my word she will be there."

"Thank you, John, and thank you, Sally," the Sheriff said. Everyone stood up, and Sally left the room. John and the Sheriff walked back to the porch, shook hands, and said good bye.

"See you Monday," the Sheriff said as he got in his car.

The Sheriff was about two miles out of town when he pulled over to the side of the road and stopped. He fumbled around under the car seat until he located his nerve medicine. He removed the lid from the fruit jar and put it to his lips. "Chug-a-lug, chug-a-lug": two good swigs. He smacked his lips and said, "That should settle my nerves. I am a nervous wreck from talking to the Ensleys." He put the jar back under the seat and headed for home. It had been a rough day for the Sheriff.

The Sheriff came to work earlier than usual on Monday morning. He called the Oak Tree Motel and reserved rooms for that night. When Bob came back from the Café, the Sheriff said, "I'm leaving to go to Haysville to get Sally and her Dad, so you will have to take care of things around here until I get back. We'll both be out of the office tomorrow. We have to be at the Judge's Office by nine. I hope this gets over with soon so I'll have time to take the Ensleys back to Haysville before dark sets in. I don't like being on the road after dark. I hope you have a good day," the Sheriff said to Bob as he left the office.

Sally and Big John were ready to leave when the Sheriff pulled into their driveway. When the Sheriff stopped the car they left the porch and came straight to the car.

"I'm shore glad you invited me to come with Sally," John said to the Sheriff. I've never been no farther than the Courthouse downtown in my whole life. Sally hadn't either until she married that Bob feller and he took her to Waynesville." Big John was really excited about the trip.

"Don't you think Sally is mighty pretty all dressed up in her church clothes?" John said.

"Mighty pretty," the Sheriff said.

"I sure hope I don't see Bob Boyd," Sally grumbled.

Big John had quieted down and was taking in all the strange and new things he saw along the road. The Sheriff didn't say anything. He was thinking about the hearing tomorrow. Sally was sulking in the corner of the backseat of the car because her Dad had made her go to Waynesville for the hearing. The trip was going real smooth, and the Sheriff was surprised and pleased.

Big John's eyes were as big as saucers when they drove into Waynesville. "Shore is a big town," he said to the Sheriff.

"We'll go to the Café and eat dinner. Then I'll take you to the motel," the Sheriff said to his guests.

When they were seated at the Café, the Sheriff said to the waiter, "Mr. Ensley and his daughter are my guests. They will be back this evening for supper and tomorrow morning for breakfast. Give them anything they want to eat and charge it to me. I'll pay you for all their meals while they are in Waynesville."

"That sure was mighty fine eating. There's nothing fancy like that in Haysville," John said.

The Sheriff drove the two blocks from the Café to the motel. He took his guests to the office to find out what room number they would be staying in. "Room 126," the clerk said as she handed the keys to the Sheriff.

John and Sally got the things they had packed for the trip and went to room 126. The Sheriff unlocked the door and handed the keys to John.

"Be sure and lock your room when you leave to go eat supper and breakfast. I'll be by tomorrow morning a little after eight to go with you to the Judge's Office. If you need anything or have any trouble, go tell the clerk at the office and they will take care of it. Get a good night's sleep," the Sheriff said as he left his guests in their room.

The next morning when he went to the motel to pick up John and Sally they were ready to go. John had shaved, combed his hair, and was wearing a pair of pants with a crease in the legs. Sally was in her church clothes and had used a little lip coloring and powder.

"My, you two look great," the Sheriff said.

When they entered the Judge's Office, the Sheriff was speechless when he saw all the people in the room. The Judge shook hands with Sally and her dad, and then he began to introduce the people in his office:

"This is a reporter from the Asheville paper. This is a reporter from the radio station in Asheville. This is the reporter from the Canton paper. This is the reporter from the Waynesville paper. This is Deputy Sheriff Bob Boyd. This is Sheriff Harbin, and our special guest is Sally Ensley and her dad, John. And I am the Judge who will hear the account of what happened to cause Bob Boyd to think he had killed his wife, Sally. All of you find a chair and sit down. Sally, you sit in the chair in front of my desk."

The Judge explained what the hearing was about and why each person was asked to be there. Sally was to tell what happened the day she went back to her dad's home. The Sheriff, Bob, and Mr. Ensley were to be witnesses to what Sally told, and all the others from the newspapers and the radio station were to get the story out to everyone by telling the true story about Bob being tried and sentenced to prison for the killing of his wife Sally and to clear the record about Bob's being a murderer.

"Sally, tell us what happened on the day that Bob was supposed to have killed you," the Judge said.

Sally turned her head and looked at everyone. She then looked straight at the Judge and began her story.

She told why she shot Ol'-Blue, Bob's hound dog and how she panicked from thinking about what Bob would do when he saw his dog. She told how she bundled the dog in the oil cloth cover from the table and how she hid by the door and hit Bob on the head with the iron skillet knocking him out. She said that she had placed the shot gun in Bob's hands, and put her clothes in a paper sack and headed toward her dad's house in Haysville.

"Is that the true account of what happened?" the Judge asked Sally.

"Yes sir," she answered.

The Judge continued by telling what went on at the trial where Bob said that he killed Sally.

"Sheriff, would you tell what happened that caused you to go looking for Sally and the truth?"

The Sheriff told how Bob was going to give what he thought was Sally a decent funeral and how curiosity got him to take a peek at what was wrapped in the table cloth and that Bob found the bones and hair of Ol' Blue, his hound dog.

"Thank you all for being here," the Judge said. "I have heard all I need to know about Bob's innocence of the charge of the murder of his wife. I'll write my ruling on this matter and send you all a copy. You are free to leave."

Everyone was moving toward the door when the Judge said, "Sheriff, I'd like to see you a minute before you leave."

When everyone was gone, the Judge said to the Sheriff, "I would like some of that good nerve medicine you usually keep. Do you think you could find some?"

"I'll take care of it as soon as I get back from Haysville. I've got to take the Ensleys home before dark. I don't want to pay another night at the motel and feed them. It'll probably be tomorrow before I can get the 'medicine.'"

"That will be fine," the Judge said.

After the Sheriff, Sally, and her dad finished eating their dinner at the Café, they left and went on their way back to Haysville. Everyone was just looking at the scenery along the road when Sally broke the silence.

"Bob sure looked handsome in his Deputy's uniform," Sally said. "I kind of feel sorry for the way I treated him. I married him, but it was awful lonely up on that mountain with no one to talk to. Bob was always off in the field working, and I was stuck in that log house all by myself. He was always promising to get a job at the tannery and move off the mountain to town."

The Sheriff and Sally's Dad didn't speak. They pretended to not have heard a thing Sally said. She quit talking and slouched down in the backseat of the car. There was very little talking for the rest of the trip.

"I shouldn't have killed his dog," Sally said. I wish now that I had stayed with him."

The Sheriff pulled his car up beside the Ensley's house and said, "Thank you for going to the hearing. I hope you enjoyed your visit to Waynesville."

"I shore enjoyed the trip, but I'm glad to be back home," Big John said. I've never been that far from home, and that's the first time I ever slept in a motel. I really liked it up there in Waynesville. I hope I can get back up there sometime. Thank you, Sheriff, for taking care of our eats and place to spend the night."

"You are welcome," the Sheriff said. "I enjoyed your company. After I retire, I'm coming to visit and go fishing again."

The Sheriff started the car up and headed toward Waynesville. "I'll be home before dark," the Sheriff said to himself."

The next morning when the Sheriff opened the door to his office, he found Bob hunkered over the little Sears radio listing to the station from Asheville. When he noticed the Sheriff he jumped up, all excited, and said, "Sheriff, you should hear what that man on the radio is saying about you and me. He's saying what a smart Sheriff you are and how you solved a murder case. Bet I don't sleep a wink until the newspapers come out." Bob was as excited as a little boy on Christmas morning.

"The Judge invited the news people so they could tell everybody that you never killed your wife Sally," the Sheriff said.

"Oh, I got so excited when I heard the radio man talking about us that I forgot to give you this letter that came yesterday," Bob said as he handed an envelope to the Sheriff.

The Sheriff held the letter up to the light as though he was trying to read it before opening the envelope.

"It's from the FBI Office over in Raleigh," said the Sheriff. He opened the envelope and read the letter.

"What do they have to say?" Bob asked.

"They said that we could use the three hundred and twenty-four dollars that we found. It doesn't belong to the bank. It must be money that the robbers got somewhere before they robbed the bank. The letter also says that the hearing for Alonzo and Shenk, the two robbers, wouldn't be held until late fall. Their lawyers had requested the delay. That's about it," said the Sheriff.

"What are you going to buy with the money?" Bob asked.

"I'm going to open a petty cash account at the bank for the Sheriff's Office. We always need a little extra money. The budget that the county sets for our office just barley gets us through every year. Sometimes I have to ask for a little extra money," the Sheriff said. "Do you want to try winning a couple of checker games?" the Sheriff asked.

ELECTION TIME

Sheriff Harbin and Deputy Bob Boyd were really happy about all the news about Bob not being guilty of killing his wife. The Sheriff's plans for Bob's future were going very well. Not only had he cleared Bob of the murder charges, but the publicity was greater than money could buy. The Judge had done some planning, also. He made sure he had people at the hearing who would get the news to the public.

After a couple of days of reading the newspapers and several checker games, the Sheriff decided that it was time to tell Bob what his plans were.

"Bob, what do you think about you taking over as the Sheriff of Haywood County?"

"I've never given it any thought. I like being a Deputy and working for you," Bob said.

"The reason that I asked is because I am thinking of retiring after this term as Sheriff. I'm sure that the new

Sheriff would hire a new Deputy, and you would be without a job," he said to Bob. "If I had a son, I would have him get on the ballot, but I have two girls, and there has never been a woman Sheriff and probably never will be one," the Sheriff said.

"Well, if I want to keep working as a lawman, I guess I'll have to be elected Sheriff. It sure would be hard for me to get elected. No one ever heard of me until my trial for killing Sally," Bob said.

"Bob, since the hearing, everyone in North Carolina knows that your trial was a mistake and that you never touched a hair on Sally's head, much less killed her. I guess you are about the best-known person there is from all the news about what happened the day you thought you killed your wife, Sally. With my help you can beat about anyone who runs against you," the Sheriff said.

"I don't even know how to get my name put on the ballot."

"Don't worry," said the Sheriff. "I'll take care of getting you certified and putting your name on the ballot. We've got to do this soon so we can do some campaigning. The sooner we start, the more people we can see."

"Do you think there will be others running for Sheriff? "Bob asked.

"Always are," the Sheriff said. "It wouldn't surprise me if one or more of them Yankees who have moved to Maggie will try getting the Sheriff's job. We've had someone who was born and raised here in Haywood as Sheriff for more than a hundred years, and I sure would hate to see an outsider take over the Sheriff's Office. Everyone knows what he can or can't do now. If someone takes over the Sheriff's job and starts changing the rules for how we do things around here, there's no telling what would happen. It could even cause trouble county-wide."

"If I'm elected as the next Sheriff, there will not be any changes in the way the law is run. The Pressley's and others who make a living by cooking a little moonshine won't have to worry about the law bothering them as long as they don't cause any trouble," Bob said.

"These people are the ones who can help most to get you elected as the next Sheriff. They all come out of the hollows on Election Day, and they all vote for the same person. They visit each other to make sure everyone knows who they will vote for come election time," the Sheriff said to Bob.

There was very little mention of the election for the rest of the week. Bob was alone most of the following days after he and the Sheriff talked about him being the next Sheriff. The Sheriff was gone most of the day, and Bob never asked him where he went or what he was doing. He figured that the Sheriff would tell him what was going on if he wanted him to know.

The following Monday the Sheriff came to the office a little earlier than usual. Bob returned from the Café where he'd eaten breakfast a few minutes after the Sheriff arrived.

"I've got something to show you," the Sheriff said to Bob.

Bob got a chair and sat down across the desk from the Sheriff.

"What are you going to show me?" Bob asked.

"See these papers," the Sheriff said. I went to the election office Monday and picked up a petition to qualify you for a place on the ballot for Sheriff when the election is held this fall. The girl in the office was surprised when I told her you were the one running for Sheriff, not me. I asked her to keep it quiet for a while. She promised me that she wouldn't tell anyone until I gave her permission.

'I'll bet I've got nearly a hundred names here from people around town who said they would support you and vote for you. Next week I'll visit all my friends who live on the mountains. I don't need all these names, but if you can get a promise from these people, you can pretty well depend on them to keep their promise. When I finish getting signatures and promises you will have to take this to the Election Office and sign it before the clerk so she can get it certified in order for your name to be on the ballot. Oh, I nearly forgot to tell you. I told the girl you would be running as a Democrat."

"Has anyone else picked up petitions for Sheriff?" Bob asked.

"No, you are the first one. You're a little early, but I wanted you to get an early start so you can see more people and get their support," the Sheriff said.

"I'll go up to Canton on the days we are not busy," Bob said. "I'll talk with the Hall and Pressley boys. If I can get them to talk to all their customers and friends, that would get a lot of votes. I'll also go to all the stores, especially those out in the community. I'll make sure that they have heard that I never killed my wife Sally."

With the plans that the Sheriff and Bob were making, the chances for Bob being the next Sheriff of Haywood County looked really good.

Another quiet week at the Sheriff's Office passed, and the Sheriff had three more pages of names for Bob to take to the Election Office in order to get his name on the ballot for the upcoming county election. Bob was getting more excited about the thoughts of him being the "High Sheriff" of Haywood County. His thoughts of finding him a girlfriend for a future wife were put on hold. He didn't have time to think about women right now.

"I guess you'd better take this petition to the Election Office and turn it in. You have to sign it so the clerk can see you signing that you are willing to be on the ballot for Sheriff. Also, ask the clerk to call you when someone else qualifies to be on the ballot for Sheriff," the Sheriff told Bob.

Everything was set for Bob to possibly be the next Sheriff of Haywood County. The papers were signed, his name was placed on the ballot, he had been to Canton and talked with the Hall and Pressley boys about helping him get votes, and the Sheriff had made several visits to his friends who lived on the ridges and in the hollows of the mountains in Haywood. The two law men were getting tired.

"Let's take a day off from campaigning and get in a game or two of checkers," the Sheriff said to Bob.

"Good idea," Bob replied. "It'll do us both good to get a little rest. I believe there is more work getting elected Sheriff than there is being a Sheriff. I'm more tired at night than I would be if I had plowed all day."

They were well into a big checker game when the telephone rang.

"Sheriff's Office. Sheriff speaking."

"Sheriff, this is Betty at the Election Office. It looks like Bob has some competition for the Sheriff's job. A fellow by the name of Mario Fotte brought in his papers for Sheriff. I asked him a few questions, and all I found out about him was that he had a gift shop over in the valley where a lot of summer visitors stay. He came to Haywood a little over a year ago from New York City and bought the shop and house. He said that he retired from the police force in New York and knew all about law enforcement. He bragged a little about the changes he would make and how he would enforce the laws. He seemed a little cocky to me. If I hear anything else, I'll call you."

"Thanks, Betty. I'll do a little checking myself," the Sheriff said.

"Do you think I have a problem with this ex-law-man?" Bob asked.

"I don't think so. Get me that letter we received from the FBI office in Raleigh. I want their phone number. I'm going to check this Mario Fotte feller out," said the Sheriff.

Bob went to the filing cabinet and got the folder marked, "Bank Robbery". He handed it to the Sheriff who opened it and found the letter from the FBI with their telephone number and address printed on it. He picked up the telephone and dialed the operator.

"Operator, this is Sheriff Harbin. Would you connect me with number 555-2626 in Raleigh? Charge the call to this phone."

"One moment please," the operator said.

Bob could hear the telephone ringing on the other end, but no one was answering. It continued to ring, and finally someone said, "FBI. Tom Henson speaking."

"Mr. Henson, this is Sheriff Harbin in Haywood County. I would like to speak with one of your agents. Is

Sam Bailey in his office?"

"Just a minute, I'll check," Henson said.

The Sheriff heard someone clearing his throat and asking who was calling him. "The Sheriff from Haywood," he heard someone answer.

"FBI. Sam Bailey here."

"Mr. Bailey, this is Sheriff Harbin over in Haywood County. I have a favor to ask of you."

"What can I do for you?" Bailey asked.

"I would like for you to get some information about a man who moved here about two years ago. He said that he retired from the police department in New York City. He operates a gift shop over in the valley where the summer visitors stay. He seems a little young to be retired. His name is Mario Fotte. I would appreciate your letting me know anything you might be able to find out about him."

"I'll see what I can do," the Agent said. "The hearing for the bank robbers should be coming up soon. Tell everyone hello for me."

"I would appreciate it if you could get this information on Fotte right away. I don't know what he is up to, but I've heard some rumors," the Sheriff said.

"I'll get right on it," said Agent Bailey.

When Bob went to the Café for dinner Fanny was already eating. When she saw Bob she motioned for him to come to her table.

"Have you seen the posters in the store windows all over town?" Fanny asked.

"What posters?" Bob asked.

"That Mario Fotee man who's running against you for the Sheriff's job is having a big barbeque over in the valley next to his shop. Everyone is invited, and it's free. He is going to tell why he would be the best Sheriff. It's all on them posters he has put up all over the County. Bet it cost a lot to have them made. There is one up front in the window. Go read it."

Bob got up from the table and went outside the Café. There in the window was the poster that Fanny was so excited about. Bob read it and went back to the table and sat down.

"Are you going," Bob asked Fanny.

"I'd like to if someone would give me a ride over there and back. I'm not interested in hearing him talk, but I sure would like some of that home cooked barbeque," Fanny said.

"I don't know if the Sheriff is planning on going," Bob said. "If he does go, I'm sure he would give you a ride."

"Just because people go and eat his barbeque doesn't mean they will vote for him," Fanny said.

When Bob returned to the Sheriff's Office, he began to tell the Sheriff about the posters and the barbeque.

"Yeah, I saw the posters this morning. I didn't mention them to you because what Fotee is doing won't get him many votes. He is spending a lot of money trying to get votes. I wonder where he gets all that money?" the Sheriff said.

"I wish I had the report on Fotee," the Sheriff said. "That may give us a clue as to where he gets all his money. He sure doesn't make a lot of money from the gift shop he runs. He only sells to the people who visit in the summer. Local people never go anywhere near the place."

The Sheriff went to the barbeque, mostly to see who was there and also to give Fanny a ride. After all, he felt that he was indebted to Fanny for helping solve the bank robbery.

When it looked like no more people would be coming to the free barbeque dinner Mario Fotte, the sponsor and Sheriff hopeful, stood up in a chair so everyone could see him and began his speech.

"Can I have your attention?" he asked the crowd of hungry people. "My name is Mario Fotee, your future Sheriff," he said to his audience. "I want to be your new Sheriff because I am the most qualified candidate, having been a police officer in the largest police department in the USA, the New York City Police Department. I know all about law enforcement. I moved here two years ago, after retirement, and I have observed how the Sheriff's Office is operated. You people deserve a more up-to-date Sheriff. One who will pay no favors to anyone, unlike the Sheriff's Office does now. I will make changes and add new rules that will clean up all the crime in Haywood County. I have the experience and education. My opponent does not have either. On Election Day, vote 'Mario Fotee' and elect the Sheriff your county deserves.

"Thank you, let's eat. Hope you enjoy the barbeque."

Fanny finished eating and said to the Sheriff, I'm ready to go home any time you are. I didn't see you eating. Weren't you hungry?"

"No," the Sheriff said.

"That feller won't get my vote just because he had free barbeque," Fanny said to the Sheriff as they were driving back to town.

The Sheriff wasn't talking very much. He had to bite his tongue to keep from saying what he was thinking about this Mr. Fotee. Especially after what he said about how he was running the Sheriff's Office and what he said about Bob not being qualified to be a good Sheriff. If Fanny wasn't riding with him he would pull over to the side of the road and take a dose of his nerve medicine that he always kept under the backseat of his car.

After dropping Fanny off at the motel where she lived and worked, the Sheriff went straight home.

"I'll need a little extra nerve medicine," the Sheriff said to himself. "It helps me go to sleep."

When Bob picked up the mail from the post office the next morning, there was a letter from the FBI office in Raleigh. He gave it to the Sheriff and anxiously waited for him to read it.

"This will bring that big-mouthed Mario Fotee down a notch or two," the Sheriff said.

"What does it say?" Bob asked the Sheriff.

The Sheriff handed Bob the letter:

Federal Bureau of Investigation
Regional Office
16 Carolina Street
Raleigh, North Carolina
Telephone: 555-2626

October 12, 1934

Buck Harbin
Sheriff, Haywood County
Waynesville, N.C.

At your request I have contacted the police department in New York City to obtain information about a former police officer of New York City who goes by the name of Mario Fotee. The following is a brief account of what I find:

Mario Fotee was employed by the New York City Police Department on January 6, 1931, as a precinct patrol officer with the rank of Rookie.

On June 16, 1932, complaints were filed by business owners on his beat. They reported that Patrolman Fotee had approached them asking for money for protection of their businesses from theft and damages from gang action.

Mr. Fotee resigned from the NYC Police Department on July 1, 1932, without notice. His present address is unknown. An investigation is still active.

The above is all the information that the New York police would release due to the nature of the crime.

If I can be of further assistance please let me know.

Sam Bailey, Agent

"Wow! Looks like Fotee was doing a little exaggerating about all the experience he has in law enforcement," Bob said. "How are we going to let everyone know the truth about the real Mr. Fotee?" Bob asked.

"I think I have a plan about how to deal with Mr. Fotee without saying anything to the people of Haywood. I'll let him tell them at his next rally," the Sheriff said.

The Sheriff didn't have to wait long to put his plan to work. The next day when Bob went to the Café for dinner the answer was in the window: another big rally for his opponent, Mr. Fotee.

"Sheriff, there is a poster in the Café window announcing a big country music show at the high school next Saturday night. There will be a band that plays on the radio over in Charlotte. And it's free for everyone. That Fotee feller is paying the band and will talk about why he should be the next Sheriff. He is shore spending a lot of money trying to get elected," Bob said.

"This is just what I've been waiting for," the Sheriff said as he took the telephone book from his desk drawer. "What's the name of that gift shop that Fotee runs?" he asked Bob.

"Don't know. Never been in his place or even close enough to see the name," Bob replied.

"This must be it. 'Mario's Gift Shop," the Sheriff said.

The Sheriff dialed a number and waited for an answer.

"Mario's Gift Shop. This is Mario. Can I help you?"

"Mr. Fotee, this is Sheriff Harbin. Would you come to my office in the courthouse as soon as you can? I need to talk with you about the election that is coming up next month." the Sheriff said.

"I can be there tomorrow morning around 9:30," said Mr. Fotee.

"That will be fine," the Sheriff answered.

He turned around and said to Bob, "It will be best if you are not around tomorrow morning when Fotee is here. You'd better hang out at the Café or somewhere until about 11:00 o'clock. He should be gone by then."

Everything was working as the Sheriff had planned: the letter from the FBI about Mr. Fotee, the rally at the school on Saturday, and Fotee agreeing to a meeting. Tomorrow would make a big difference in who would be elected Sheriff of Haywood County. The Sheriff had a grin on his face bigger than a possum's.

The next morning Mr. Fotee was on time for his appointment with the Sheriff. The Sheriff had all his words memorized, and he was ready to expose Mr. Fotee as a liar and a phony.

After greeting each other the Sheriff said to Fotee, "Have a seat."

"What do you want to see me about?" Fotee asked.

"As you should know, as Sheriff of Haywood County I took an oath in which I swore to protect the people of this county, not only from physical harm, but also from being misled by false promises that would cause them grief. It is also my duty to investigate anyone who is running for an office of the county government. I need to ask you a few questions."

"That's fine with me. Go ahead and ask me anything you like," Fotee said.

"First, how long have you lived in Haywood County?"

"Nearly two years," Fotee answered.

"Where did you live before moving here?"

"New York City," he said.

"What kind of work did you do in New York?"

"I was a police officer, which is a big plus for me being the Sheriff of this County. I am well qualified from all the experience I gained while on the police force of the largest city in this country."

"How long were you on the police force in New York?"

"I can't recall exactly, but it was for several years," Fotee replied.

It was time for the Sheriff to make the big play that he was waiting on. He took some papers from the drawer of his desk and shuffled through them. He put them all back into his desk except one, which he pretended to read.

"I want you to read a letter I have here," the Sheriff said as he handed it to Mr. Fotee.

After reading the letter that the Sheriff received from the FBI, Mario Fotee asked, "What are you trying to do to me?"

"As I told you at the beginning of our meeting, I took an oath to protect the people of the county, and I'm doing just that by exposing you as a liar and a phony. You lied to the people at the barbeque about your being an expert lawman. After I received this letter, your reputation bothered me very much. Who knows? If you were Sheriff, would you run a protection racket with the businesses in Haywood County as you did in New York?"

Fotee stood up and was about to leave without saying a word.

"I have one more thing to say to you," the Sheriff said. "I could hold you and notify the New York police, but I won't until they ask me to do so. It wouldn't surprise me if they do.

"And when you talk to the people at the country music show this Saturday, you tell them the truth about your experience as a lawman. Or would you like for me to read this letter to them?"

Fotee didn't say a thing, and he left as fast as he could.

As the week went by there was lots of talk and excitement about the big country music show coming up on Saturday night at the high school. The Sheriff had plans to attend and hear what Fotee had to say to the people at the country show.

On Saturday the Sheriff went home after Bob came back from eating dinner at the Café. He told Bob that if he was needed to call him at home.

At 4:30 Bob had a visitor at the office. The manager of the country show introduced himself to Bob.

"My name is Al Horn. I am trying to locate Mr. Fotee. He wasn't at the school or at his shop over in the valley. He promised to pay me for putting on the country show at the school tonight. Do you know where I might find him?" he asked Bob.

"No, I don't. But I'll call the Sheriff. He may know," Bob said.

Bob picked up the telephone and called the Sheriff and told him about Al Horn looking for Fotee. When he finished talking to the Sheriff, he said to Al, "Pull up a chair and sit down. The Sheriff will be here in a few minutes to talk with you. He didn't tell me anything other than have you wait until he comes to the office."

About thirty minutes passed, and the Sheriff arrived. He shook hands with Al and said, "I went by the gift shop that Fotee owns over in the valley, and it was locked up. I asked a couple of people if they knew where he was, and they said the shop had been closed all week and that they hadn't seen Fotee since Tuesday or Wednesday. You may as well get your band together and head back to Charlotte. I don't think you will find him anytime soon."

"Who is going to pay me for coming all the way from Charlotte?" Al asked the Sheriff.

"You will have to find Fotee to get your money. He is the one you have the contract with," the Sheriff said.

Al Horn left the Sheriff's Office shaking his head saying that he may as well go tell the boys that the show was canceled.

The Sheriff left for home. Bob locked the office and went to the Café to eat his supper. Bob was trying to figure out everything that had taken place in the last few days. He wondered where his opponent, Mario Fotee, could have gone.

OFFICE CHANGES

When the Sheriff came to the office on Monday morning, he was all smiles. He was accomplishing what he had planned: getting Bob elected Sheriff of Haywood County so he could retire. It seemed that Bob's only competition had left Haywood County after the meeting with the Sheriff.

The election would be held two weeks from Thursday. The time had expired for other candidates to get their names on the ballot. The only names on the ballot for Sheriff were Bob Boyd and Mario Fotee. Everything looked good for Bob. Fotee had disappeared, the much advertised country show was canceled without notice, and all the people who went to the high school on Saturday night were told there would not be a show. They were mad at Fotee.

After Bob returned from dinner at the Café, the Sheriff asked him to have a seat across the desk from him.

"Bob, I'm sure you have noticed how fast our county is growing since you started as the first Deputy of Haywood County, especially over in the valley. Two new motels, a new eating place they call a restaurant, and several new gift shops have opened in the last year. Not only is the valley crowded in the summer months, Waynesville is getting more visitors, also. As I see it, the Sheriff's Office needs to be larger in the future. I have talked to the County Commissioners about this, and after the election I will meet with them again before I leave the Sheriff's Office. This office needs at least two full-time Deputies and a Clerk to answer the phone and type the reports. During the summer months you should have a full-time Deputy over in the valley. I'm telling you this so you can begin making plans and thinking about who you could get to take these jobs. I'll work for you as a Deputy until you can find two Deputies and a Clerk. I will also help you when you need extra help after I retire."

"I've not been elected Sheriff yet, but I sure thank you for all the advice you are giving me," Bob said. "I'll start looking around for some people who would make good Deputies."

"It's not too early to start looking," the Sheriff said.

"I may be a little late coming back to the office after eating dinner," Bob said. "I'm going to talk to someone about being a Deputy if I am elected Sheriff."

Bob was eating his dinner at the table with Fanny, the girl who did the maid work at the motel.

"Fanny, is your boss working today?" he asked.

"Do you mean Mr. Owens?" she asked.

"Yeah, Al Owens, the manager," Bob said.

After Bob and Fanny finished eating, they walked to

the motel together. Al Owens, the manager, was at the check-in desk when Bob entered the motel.

"Mr. Owens, do you have time to talk with me for a few minutes?" Bob asked.

"Sure. As soon as the Desk Clerk gets back. She'll be here any minute now," he answered.

When the Desk Clerk returned, Al said to Bob, "Let's go into my office where it's quiet."

"What's on your mind?" Al asked Bob.

"I may be a little early with my planning for changes in the Sheriff's Office before I'm elected Sheriff, but I want to ask if you would be a full-time Deputy if I become Sheriff. I have plans to keep a Deputy over in the valley full-time, and you being around visitors from out-of-town while working here at the motel would make you the perfect person to be this Deputy. I don't know what the pay will be, but I'll try to give you as much as you earn here at the motel, or more."

"Do I have to give you my answer now?" Al asked. "I'll have to think it over for a few days."

"No. Think about it for a few days and let me know. I would like for you to tell me now if you are interested in the job."

"I'm definitely interested in being a Deputy. I have been ever since I was a temporary Deputy when we caught the bank robbers. Sure was exciting. All I hear around here is complaints from the workers or the guests. The workers want more money, and the guests always want more towels or something. These summer visitors are never satisfied. I'll let you know by next Monday whether I'll take the job."

"That will be soon enough," Bob said. "Sure hope you

decide to join me in the Sheriff's Office."

Bob had made his first contact in getting the right people to work in the Office of the Sheriff. He would make the next contact as soon as he thought of someone. That someone came as a surprise to Bob. It was when he was eating with Fanny at the Café that out of the blue he stopped eating, looked straight at Fanny and said, "Fanny, have you ever given any thought to working somewhere besides the motel?"

"You couldn't count on your hands and toes how many times I've thought of quitting. I get awful tired of cleaning floors and making beds day after day. I would have quit a long time ago, but jobs are scarce here in Waynesville. I don't want to move to somewhere else, and I have to work if I stay here. Why do you ask?" she said.

"I'm making plans to have more people working in the Sheriff's Office if I am elected Sheriff. I would like to have two more people, and maybe three. I also want someone in the office to answer the phone, type reports, and keep the filing up-to-date. Can you type?"

"I took typing in high school and made good grades in it," Fanny said.

"Would you like to be considered for the Clerk's job in the Sheriff's Office?" Bob asked Fanny.

"I sure would," Fanny answered.

"Fanny, I'm asking you not to mention this to anyone until I am sure the County will authorize these extra people on the Sheriff's payroll. And, if your boss at the motel found out that you may leave, he would start looking for someone to take your job. Best that no one finds out that you may leave the motel job."

"I'll keep quiet about it", she said.

When Bob returned to the office from the Café, the Sheriff was busy sorting through some papers. Bob pulled up a chair beside the desk and sat down.

"Sheriff, can I bother you for a few minutes?" Bob asked.

"Sure. What do you want?" asked the Sheriff.

"Remember your telling me to start looking around for more help here at the office if I am elected Sheriff? Well, I've talked to a couple of people, and they are to let me know if they would take the jobs. I talked to Al Owens, the motel manager who we used as a temporary Deputy during the bank robbery case, about being a Deputy and to Fanny, the cleaning girl at the motel, about taking a job as Secretary here in the office."

"Two good choices," said the Sheriff.

"I've been thinking that it would be good for the Sheriff's Office to have a Deputy from the other end of the county. One from around Canton," Bob said.

"Good Idea," said the Sheriff.

"Could I have the car one day to drive up to Canton and check around and talk to a few people about being a Deputy Sheriff for Haywood County?" Bob asked.

"Sure, any day this week. It's pretty quiet around here at the present. What day?" the Sheriff asked.

"Tomorrow would be fine," Bob said.

Bob went to the Café for breakfast earlier than usual the next morning and was back at the office when the Sheriff came to work.

"If it's all right with you, I'll drive up to Canton this morning," Bob said. I'll get an early start and try to be back sometime after dinner."

The Sheriff handed Bob the keys for the Model-A

Ford and said, "No need to hurry. Take your time and find the right person to be a good Deputy."

Bob was on his way to Canton, and there was no question as where he would go first and who he would talk to first: Brad Hall and Paul Pressley his new friends he met while working on the Bluebird Gang case. They were the two young moonshine haulers and bootleggers who lived on Home Brew Knob. He was pretty sure that they were driven to this kind of work because they couldn't find employment elsewhere.

Bob had only been to Home Brew Knob once, but he was pretty sure of how to get there. Around the river, right on the first road at the top of Crossroad Hill, then the third house on the left.

"Hope they are home," Bob said to himself. "They're home. Both cars are there beside the house."

Bob parked his car and went to the front door and knocked. Brad opened up and said, "Paul, we've got company. Guess who?"

When Paul came to the door and saw Bob he smiled and said, "Well, if it ain't old Bob, the feller who thought he killed his wife a while back. Come in and visit awhile."

After the hand shaking and pats on the back, they all sat down in the living room.

"What are you doing in that Sheriff's car?" Paul asked.

"I am a Deputy Sheriff of Haywood County, and I'm running for Sheriff. That is why I came to see you. I'm looking for a good man to be one of my Deputies if I am elected Sheriff. Either of you interested in the job?" Bob asked.

"You must be kidding. A bootlegger being a law

man?" Brad said.

"Nothing wrong with that. I got a chance to prove my worth after I got out of jail. Everybody deserves a second chance," Bob said.

"I was thinking about you, Brad. Your being from Canton, hardly anyone knows you around Waynesville. Do you think you would be interested?" Bob asked.

"What about Paul? He couldn't operate alone," Brad said.

"I figured he could go back to Waynesville and help his dad. He's getting kind of feeble, according to what the Sheriff tells me. He visits the Pressley's a lot, especially when he runs low on his 'nerve medicine.'"

"We'll talk it over and let you know before the election," Brad said.

"That will be fine with me. I hope you decide to join me," Bob said. "I hate to leave so soon, but I got to get the Sheriff's car back to the Sheriff," Bob said as he was leaving.

Bob thought he'd better talk to someone else before going back to Waynesville just in case Brad didn't want to become a Deputy Sheriff. He remembered his dad telling him about a man by the name of Wesley Stone who lived up on Beaverdam Mountain and was a long-time lawman and a good one. He had a large family and there were several boys. Bob decided to pay them a visit and see if one of them is qualified and interested in a career in the Sheriff's Office. They surely learned something from their dad.

After asking directions to the house where the Stones lived, Bob found their log house about half way up the mountain beside a narrow dirt road. The door was open, and when Bob was close to the house a lanky boy who looked to be in his early twenties met him on the porch. He glanced at the car and saw the Sheriff's star on it.

"Howdy, Sheriff," he said. "What brings you up here?"

"I'm not the Sheriff. I'm a Deputy Sheriff, but I may be the Sheriff after the election next week. That is why I'm here. I'd like to talk with you and your brothers. I heard a lot about your dad being a good Constable for many years before he passed away. I'm hoping some of his good work rubbed off on you and that you might like to be a law man."

"Dad talked a lot about his job to us before he died and sort of wanted one of us to carry on the work he was doing. Me being the oldest boy in the family, I guess I should look into becoming a lawman just like him. I'm twenty-two years old next month."

"If I win the Sheriff's job and there is an opening for a Deputy's job in the Sheriff's Office, would you be interested in becoming a Deputy? I'm not promising you a job. I just want to have someone in mind if I need another man."

"I'd sure like to have the job if you ever need me. My name is Jim, Jim Stone."

"I'll come back to see you when I need someone," Bob said to Jim. "I've got to get back to Waynesville. I would appreciate you getting me all the votes you can next week."

When Bob opened the door to the Sheriff's Office, he saw that the Sheriff was leaning back in his swivel chair with his eyes closed. When Bob shut the door, he jumped up and was wide awake.

"You scared the daylights out of me," he said to Bob. "I sort of dozed off a little. It's awful quiet when you're not around. Did you do any good up in Canton?" he asked Bob.

"I sure did. I have two prospects for the Deputy's job if I need anyone." He didn't tell the Sheriff who they were. "Everything is all set. There's nothing else to do until after the election," Bob said.

After several checker games and a few short sitting-up naps, it was Election Day. Bob borrowed the Sheriff's car and went to every voting place in Haywood County. He wanted to meet the voters who had never seen him.

It was a long day for Bob. It was midnight before all the votes were counted, and Bob wouldn't know the results until the next day. The votes were sorted and counted by hand.

As soon as the Election Office opened the next morning, Bob was first in line to hear the results. As expected, Bob received nearly one hundred percent of the votes for the next Sheriff of Haywood County. His opponent, Mr. Fotee, wasn't seen or heard from on Election Day.

Bob went back to the Sheriff's Office. He was excited and also worried about how he would do in his new job. But he was pleased to know that the Sheriff was helping him get going before leaving for his retirement.

"Bob, the County Commissioners meet Monday, and you and I will be there. There were several new men elected to the Commission, and that Smith feller who was always voting against everything got beat and won't be there. We have to get you enough money in the budget so you can hire the extra Deputies that this County needs. My guess is that the county has two hundred more people than it had when I became Sheriff. And business is growing by leaps and bounds over in the valley.

We'll get that money. You watch and see," he said to Bob.

RETIRED

Although he had looked forward to retiring and doing nothing but hanging around the Courthouse, the
long-time Sheriff of Haywood County, Paul Harbin, had
mixed feelings about his retirement. He was giving some
thought to buying some fishing equipment and paying a visit to his friend Big John Ensley at the lake near
Haysville. Big John Ensley knew where all the good fishing places were in that big lake between North Carolina
and Georgia.

He also had plans for doing a bit more visiting with
his favorite friend, Ben Pressley. Another of Ben's sons
had decided to help out with the business, so he and his
friend Ben could take all the time to visit with each other
that they wanted now that both of them were retired. After all, Ben was retired Sheriff Paul Harbin's best supplier
of what he referred to as his "headache medicine". It was
the best corn likker that could be found. Ben had taught
his sons well how to follow the traditions that he was
taught by his father before him.

As retired Sheriff Paul Harding sat in a chair near the

checker board, his mind moved in all directions thinking about all that had taken place while he was the former Sheriff -- especially all that had happened with his
good friend and the newly-elected Sheriff, Bob Boyd.
He wouldn't try to remember or count all of the checker
games he had played since he became the first Deputy
Sheriff of Haywood County. Nor could he forget the
blunder he made when Bob said he had killed his wife
Sally. He never attempted to investigate the murder. Bob
was tried and had to spend a year in jail although he
hadn't committed any crime. The Sheriff regretted that
he hadn't taken the time to see if Bob was actually guilty
of murder. But he was proud of having a hand in guiding
Bob all the way from the first paid Deputy to the elected
Sheriff of Haywood County. There was a smile of satis-
faction on his face for having a Sheriff in the family. Bob
had been the son that Sheriff Harding never had. All of
his children were girls.

The ex-Sheriff remembered how he had planned for
the Federal agents to catch one of the local bootleggers
so the Revenuers would move on to another county. He
often thought of Ben Pressley, his most trusted and best
friend. He recalled the many times he had asked Ben
for advice. He thought of how he had kept the peace between all the other families who were in the moonshine
business in the hollers and on the ridges of North Carolina. And, of course, he knew that he could always depend
on Ben for his headache medicine. (Even the Judge who
presided over the criminal court of the county was now
also a good customer of Ben Pressley's.)

Sheriff Harding directed his attention to where Bob
was sitting by the desk near Fanny, the new secretary for

the Sheriff's Office. The retiring Sheriff had forgotten that Bob was in the room. His mind had been carried away thinking of the years that he had been in office as the Sheriff of Haywood County. He moved over to the chair sitting across from Bob and Fanny.

"Ever heard anything about the two men who robbed the bank?" he asked Bob.

"I was planning to tell you about the call I received from the FBI agent the other day. I've been all carried away getting the Office in order. There's sure more work now than when we ran the Office. Agent Bailey from the district office of the FBI told me that the trial for the bank robbers was held a couple of weeks ago. That feller called Alonzo was sentenced to prison for three years, and the other one, called Shenk, got two years in prison. Seems that the feller called Alonzo was the leader when they robbed the bank up here in Waynesville. Agent Bailey told me that they didn't need any of us from here in Waynesville to come as witnesses for the trial."

"I haven't seen your new Deputies around," the retired Sheriff said.

"I have Owens over in the Valley. That place is growing by leaps and bounds. We had ten new people move there this summer. They are buying land like you wouldn't believe. Seems they want to build their houses in the highest and steepest places they can find. You couldn't even grow a garden where they build, it's so steep and rocky. I don't think they've ever seen a rock pile."

"Where's your other Deputy?"

"You must mean the young bootlegger I hired, Brad Hall. I have him working all around the county. He uses the new car that the county let us buy. It sure comes in handy. Haywood is a pretty big area. If he didn't have the car, Brad couldn't do the job like it should be done. Our work's keeping everyone busy. I doubt I'll get in any checkers since you are leaving."

"How is the Secretary working out?" he asked Bob.

"You mean Fanny?"

"She's the only one I see," the ex-Sheriff said.

"It has been a while since she had done any typing, but she's getting the hang of it. We don't have a lot of typing. It's mostly answering the 'phone, keeping records, and filing. You would never believe all the records the Government wants us to keep."

After the retired Sheriff had checked out the new employees who Bob hired for the Sheriff's Office, he was relieved that he was retiring. He liked the old way of running the Sheriff's Office. He was never one for keeping records. Having to keep records made him feel like people didn't trust each other.

The old Sheriff got up from his chair, shook hands with Bob, and started on his way out of the Office. Before he left, he said, "I won't be bothering you too much, but if you get in tight place and need a little help every now and then, you give me a call. I'll be glad to give you a hand."

Having said that, he left the office. He was now officially retired.

A NEW DAY

The election was over. Bob was elected the new Sheriff of Haywood County. The county government approved the request to hire three more employees for the Sheriff's Office and also money to purchase another patrol car for the new Deputies. The Sheriff's Office was changing and fast becoming one of the best law enforcement departments in Western North Carolina and maybe the best one.

Al Owens, the motel manager, was hired as a Deputy Sheriff. He resigned as manager of the motel. Brad Hall, the young bootlegger from Canton, was also hired as a new Deputy Sheriff. Fanny, the cleaning girl from the motel, was hired as the Secretary for the Sheriff's Office. Bob had hopes of hiring the Stone boy from Beaverdam as a Deputy for the Canton area later if he could convince the county government of the need for a Deputy in that end of the county. The Sheriff's Office staff was now double what it had been before Bob was elected Sheriff, and they also had two patrol cars.

"Bob, I'll stay a few days and help you get everything

going before I retire," the Sheriff said.

"Thanks, Sheriff. I need all the help I can get until I get the hang of being Sheriff," Bob said.

The next day after eating dinner Bob told Al, the new Deputy, "I'll be gone for a while, so you take over while I'm gone."

Bob went to the office of Valley Real Estate over near Lake Junaluska. The Methodist Church sent delegates to their place on the lake for an annual meeting every summer. Some of these out-of-town people bought land and built a second home in Haywood County. Bob wanted to sell his mountain place and get a house near the City of Waynesville. He asked a real estate agent if he could help him find a buyer for his mountain place.

"How much mountain land do you own?" the real estate agent asked Bob.

"I don't know right off. My daddy gave me the land before he died. It must be over fifty acres of land, and there's a house with two bedrooms, a sitting room, and a kitchen. The place also has a barn with stalls for cows and horses and a hay loft. I had a cow, a horse, chickens, and a coon dog. My wife killed my dog, and I don't know what went with the cow, horse, and chickens since I moved to town," Bob told the agent.

"How much money are you asking for your place?" the agent asked.

"I don't have any idea," Bob answered.

"When can you go with me and let me take a look at your place?" the agent asked.

"We could go now if you have the time," he answered.

The agent and Bob went to see the land and house

that Bob wanted to sell. They had to walk from the main road up the sled road to get there.

The agent took a good look around the house and then opened the door and went inside. It was what Bob had told him: sitting room, cooking and eating room, and two bedrooms. He hadn't told the agent that you had to climb a ladder up to the loft to the second bedroom.

"The land lies pretty well. This house isn't the best but also not the worst I've seen. It would make a good vacation home," the agent said.

"I'll have it surveyed to see how many acres you have and then set a selling price. You probably could get two hundred and maybe a little more an acre," he said. "I'll charge you three percent of what I get for your place" he added.

As they rode back to the real estate office in the valley, Bob said, "When I sell my place, I will buy a house in town to be close to the Sheriff's Office."

"There is a two bedroom house for rent out toward the hospital if you want to rent, and the owner may sell it to you later," the agent said.

"Would you give me the address, and I'll go look at it. It may be what I'm looking for," Bob said.

When Bob returned to the office and asked if anything had happened while he was away the answer was, "No".

"I'm teaching Brad how to play checkers," Al said.

Everything had gone smoothly for Bob and his staff since he was sworn as the new Sheriff. There hadn't been any major crimes. They had only a few arrests on the weekends for drinking too much moonshine. There was a fight every now and then, and Bob had to go to court on Mondays to press charges against the weekend lock-ups.

These weekend disturbances were usually caused by the summer visitors from down south or up north, not by the natives of Haywood County.

Bob rented the house near the hospital, bought a little furniture, and moved from his home at the jail. He continued to eat his meals at the Café but not with Fanny. She usually ate with Brad since he became one of the new Deputies. Fanny had her eyes on him from the first day she saw him.

Although Bob loved his job as Sheriff, there was something missing in his life. He had started thinking about the wife he brought to Waynesville from Haysville, what took place on the mountain. He remembered seeing her at the hearing before the Judge to clear his name for his murder conviction and how pretty she looked all dressed up and her pretty red hair. He was tired of being a bachelor and living alone.

The more he thought of Sally, the more he thought about the things he should and should not have done when he was married to her. He took her to the log house on the mountain where she never saw anyone but him, and that was late in the evening when he returned from the fields where he had been farming. It had been just her and the animals all day long. She had no one to talk to, and she was afraid of Ol' Blue, and he didn't like Sally because she was always hitting him with the broom to keep him out of the house. Making her live that way was not the right way to treat a pretty young girl. "I would do things differently if I had another chance," he thought to himself. "Maybe I'll go over to Haysville and have a talk with her."

A few days later Bob said to Al, "Al, I will be gone

most of the day tomorrow, and you will be in charge of the office until I get back. Do you think you can handle it?" he asked.

"Sure. Go on, and don't worry. I'll be fine," Al said.

Bob got up early the next morning for an early start for his drive over to Haysville to talk with Sally. He shaved, polished his shoes, and laid out his clean, pressed uniform the night before. After washing his face and hands, he put some rose oil on his hair. He had bought it at the five-and-dime store the evening before so he would look especially sharp when he saw Sally. He skipped his breakfast at the Café. He was anxious to get on his way.

It seemed to Bob that it was a longer trip this time than it was the time he went to Haysville looking for a wife. He knew exactly where Sally lived although he had only been there once.

When Bob arrived at the Ensley house, he saw Ben in his usual place: the rocking chair on the front porch. Ben didn't recognize Bob until he was on the porch.

"Well, look who's here. Sally's husband, the Deputy Sheriff from Waynesville," Ben said.

"I'm not a Deputy Sheriff anymore. I am the Sheriff of Haywood County," Bob said. "Good to see you again, Mr. Ensley. I would like to talk with Sally if I can. Is she home?"

"Sally. Someone's here to see you. Come out here," Ben said in a loud voice.

Sally came out onto the porch, and when she saw Bob she was speechless. She had an apron on and her pretty red hair was not combed. She was embarrassed when she saw Bob all dressed up in his Sheriff's uniform.

"S-s-ally," Bob stuttered. "I would like to talk with

you if there is somewhere we can be alone and if you will talk with me."

"I've looked for you about every day since I was in Waynesville to see the Judge," Sally said. "Let's go sit on the swing under the maple tree out in the yard so no one can hear what we talk about."

As soon as Sally and Bob were seated in the swing, Bob reached out and held Sally's hand. He began by telling her about being the new Sheriff. About selling the house on the mountain and having a house in town. Bob stuttered again as he was searching for words to tell Sally why he really came to see her.

"S-s-ally, since the day you came to Waynesville I've been thinking how I treated you when we were married and I took you to live on the side of that old mountain. I've never stopped thinking of you, and I don't hardly blame you for killing Ol' Blue, packing up, and coming back to your dad's. I want to tell you I am sorry that I took you to that lonely place to be by yourself most of the time. We are still married. I still love you, and I'm asking you to go back to Waynesville with me. I want to start a new life with you."

Bob noticed a tear running down Sally's cheek. She looked straight at him and said, "I've felt the same way about you every day since the hearing. I still love you, too, and I am sorry for what I did that day when I killed your dog and hit you with the frying pan. I've looked every day hoping you would come back for me. I even went to the preacher over at the Baptist Church and asked him what to do. He told me to be patient, and if you did come to forgive you.

"Yes, Bob. You are still my husband, and I will go

back to Waynesville to start our lives all over."

"I'll sit with your dad while you get whatever you want to take with you."

Sally and Bob were soon on their way, and they had never sat this close together before. Sally was sitting in the middle of the car seat as close as she could get to Bob. He was driving a lot slower returning to Waynesville than he was that morning. They were two happy young people who still loved each other.

It had been over a year since Sally and Bob were back together as man and wife, and the family was larger. Sally and Bob were the proud parents of a healthy baby boy with bright red hair, the same as Sally's. Bob had good people helping him with the Sheriff's job. He had hired three good people who didn't have any experience in law enforcement, including a young ex-bootlegger, Brad Hall. Bob wanted to give him a chance for a better life.

There had not been any major crimes in the county since Bob became Sheriff. The tradition of the Sheriff's Office being handed down to the son of the former son had been broken. The way of life for the people who lived in Western North Carolina was changing fast because of new people coming from all over to make their homes there. All those who lived in this mountain town were seeing the lifestyle and the traditions that they once knew change. For Haywood County, North Carolina, it was a new day.

AUTHOR'S NOTE

I do not see myself as an author but as more of a writer and storyteller. I wrote this book, *The Sheriff,* as a fiction based on hearing the older people talk about the news when I was growing up in the Canton area of Haywood County, North Carolina. The main source of communication in those days was passing news from one person to another with a little more drama added each time it was told.

As the writer, I also added some to the events but not to the extent that they could not have happened as I tell them. I write my stories to try and give the reader the impression that they are listening to me tell them, and my publisher honors my request to publish the book in this form.

I hope you enjoyed reading this book as much as the eighty-eight year old author did writing it.

Charles C Fletcher
July 2010

The author, Charles C Fletcher has published three other books
Out West and Back, The Panther on Cold Mountain and Other Stories and Little Sam Mountain.

The stories in Charles Fletcher's books are from his memories of his growing up in the mountains of Western North Carolina.

www.ingramcontent.com/pod-product-compliance
Lightning Source LLC
Chambersburg PA
CBHW070954120726
47910CB00004B/1235